THE HOBBY SHOP ON BARNABY STREET

Homefront Hearts #1

Jillianne Hamilton writes delightful historical fiction and historical romance featuring rebellious women and happy endings. Her debut novel was shortlisted for the PEI Book Award and her debut historical fiction novel was longlisted for the Historical Fiction Company Book Award. She lives in Charlottetown on Canada's east coast.

OTHER BOOKS BY THE AUTHOR

The Spirited Mrs. Pringle
The Seamstress on Cider Lane
The Land Girl on Lily Road

The Lazy Historian's Guide to the Wives of Henry VIII

Molly Miranda: Thief for Hire
Molly Miranda: Thick as Thieves
Molly Miranda: Honor Among Thieves

The Hobby Shop on Barnaby Street
By Jillianne Hamilton

www.Jilly.ca

ISBN: 978-1-7752560-8-3

Published in 2022 by Jillianne Hamilton and Tomfoolery Press.

Book and cover design by Jillianne Hamilton.

the Hobby Shop on Barnaby Street

A HOMEFRONT HEARTS NOVEL

TFP

one

Maisie

"Have you heard from Roy?"

"How is Roy?"

"Roy is certainly a brave chap, isn't he? You must be so proud."

Not a single shift went by at Hazeldon's village shop without a handful of customers asking about my brother. Before the war he was known for being charming, handsome, and athletic. Now he was a Navy hero too.

Despite Roy's infrequent letters home, I always made sure curious patrons knew he was doing well. Then, in return, I would ask them about their husband, brother, son, or cousin. So many of us were missing our menfolk, except for the lucky lads who were farmers or in another reserved occupation.

Mr. Barker, a retired professor and one of my favorite customers, popped into the shop late one summer afternoon, a camera bag slung over his shoulder.

"Good afternoon, Miss Maisie," he said, placing two tins on the counter; one for tea and one for pipe tobacco. "Any news of your brother recently?"

"We received a letter from him yesterday, actually," I said, punching the buttons on the cash register. "He's doing very well."

Mr. Barker's eyes narrowed behind his round spectacles and he tapped his ruddy cheek. "What was he doing before the war?"

"He co-owns a hobby shop in London."

"Oh, that's right," he said in his gentle Welsh lilt, the warmth suddenly fading from his expression. "Jean was supposed to work there."

Hearing her name was jarring. It was rare for anyone in Hazeldon to mention Aunt Jean or, if they did, they just didn't do it in front of my family. Mr. Barker used to be a chum of hers, developing her pictures and exchanging photography tips with her.

Anxious to change the subject, I gestured to his camera bag. "You picked a fine day to go on an excursion. Are you still using the same Kodak?"

"Aye. It's served me well this long. No reason to trade it in yet." He eyed me curiously. "Have you ever considered taking up the hobby again? You were very good as I recall."

"No." I shrugged. "Just lost interest in it, I suppose."

"Mmm," he said, dropping his gaze. "Well, that can happen." He looked back up at me, his wide crinkled smile not quite reaching his eyes. "I used to like fishing. I haven't picked up my fishing pole in ages." He chuckled.

I hadn't taken a single photograph since Jean's accident.

Shortly after Mr. Barker left, a shipment of canned goods came in and I went about stocking shelves with Doris, the shop assistant. Doris was a little older than me with a younger sister who was in my class at school. She was a good employee, but I was confident she only took the job because the village shop was always the best place to hear the juiciest gossip.

"I told you about my sister getting a job as a typist for the government, right?" She slid a can of green beans onto the shelf overhead. "I got a letter from her yesterday. She met Mr. Churchill!"

"Really? Was he nice?"

"I don't think they had a conversation or anything. I think she was delivering something to his offices and he said hello." Doris shrugged.

"Knowing her, she'll put it on her résumé."

"Does she like living in London?"

"I think so. She's getting a little nervous about the raids though. The BBC makes it sound like the Nazis are going to start dropping bombs there any day." Doris moved some older cans to the front of the shelf and placed newer cans in behind them. "At least we don't have to worry about that here."

"Can you mash the potatoes for me, dear?" Mum yelled the moment I stepped through the front door after my shift.

And hello to you too.

"Sure," I called back, slipping off my shoes and hurrying to join her in the kitchen. "Smells good in here."

She rolled her eyes at me and fetched the dinner plates from the cupboard. "I can't wait for this war to be over so I don't have to think about food rations ever again."

"That's what our boys *are* fighting for." I said with a smirk. "So we won't have to use ration coupons any longer."

Mum, ignoring my remark, whipped around the kitchen like a trout through a stony brook while I hammered at the potatoes with the masher, pushing down hard to get the lumps out.

"I spent the afternoon raising money for the Spitfire Fund," Mum said, stopping for a moment to catch her breath. "Begging more like it. People are pinching their pennies a lot more than they used to when the war first started."

"Understandable," I said. "Everything is so uncertain right now."

"I wish you were home more to help me with chores and meals," she said dismissively. "You *should* be home more. Surely your father can find someone else to manage the shop."

I was used to this line. I'd been working at the village shop since I was sixteen. I'd become the most senior employee at the shop when the former manager signed up for the Royal Air Force. Meanwhile, Dad spent most of his time bouncing between his two larger, busier shops in Guildford, the town closest to Hazeldon.

"Dad depends on me. You know that," I said, scooping potatoes into the serving dish.

Mum huffed, wrinkling her nose and pursing her lips in disgust. She disappeared into the dining room in a blur of sky-blue gingham, muttering something about "a daughter's duties" under her breath.

Dad arrived home soon after and the three of us sat down to dinner. He and I made our usual small talk about shop stuff—mostly shipping delays and customers asking for items we couldn't get because of supply chain issues. Keeping a shop's shelves full in 1940 was much more of a challenge than we were used to.

Dad chewed thoughtfully. "I heard people are forging ration books to sell them on the black market. Some ration books have even been stolen." He shook his head.

I glanced at Mum, silently wondering if she would ever consider buying a forged or stolen ration book.

She wouldn't dare. She'd rather go to war personally than be known as a criminal around the village.

"I was thinking about Roy's letter from yesterday." Dad sipped his tea. "He said Calvin lost another employee at the hobby shop. Another defector to munitions factory work."

Cal, Roy's best friend from childhood, co-owned the hobby shop in London. He was left to run the shop by himself once Roy signed up for the Navy. None of Cal's hires seemed to last very long—they either found higher paying jobs elsewhere or they left the city to avoid the impending raids.

I couldn't say I blamed them.

"I think I might try to help him out a few times a week," Dad said nonchalantly. "I can take the train to London and back until he finds someone else—"

"George, you are far too busy with the business to think about that," Mum said, her eyes stern. "Calvin can manage. It's not your concern."

Dad's thick eyebrows kneaded together, his frown tight.

True, the shop *wasn't* Dad's responsibility, but I could tell he felt obligated to do *something* about it. Dad had purchased a London hardware store seven years ago and he and his Bohemian younger sister Jean converted it to a hobby shop where they could sell cameras, scrapbooking ephemera, stamp collecting supplies, and other leisure products. Jean could also develop pictures in the basement photography lab. The hobby shop was Dad's way of giving Jean a more stable income than freelance photography could provide.

Three days before the hobby shop was to open, Jean was doing some nature photography and slipped on a rocky cliff edge, falling to her death.

I was fifteen. Not only did I admire and adore my aunt, but I also idolized her completely. She taught me everything she knew about photography, generous with her knowledge and an enthusiastic teacher.

Dad went ahead with the opening of the hobby shop without Jean but hired people to manage and work for him. Being there reminded him of her.

After several years Dad gave up the hobby shop. Even though Roy never once had an interest in working retail, my brother jumped at the chance to get out of Hazeldon and move to London. Dad handed him the keys and wished him well.

Giving the shop to me was never brought up. I often wondered if the thought crossed his mind even once.

Dad lowered his teacup. "I think I better go up and help him—"

"Maisie can go."

With my mouth full of food and my eyes wide, I slowly turned to Mum. "Hmm?"

Mum smiled sweetly at me. "You can go to London and work at the shop for a while, can't you?"

I swallowed. "But who would manage the village shop if I'm in London?"

"Doris, obviously."

"Are you serious? Have you *met* Doris? She's lovely but a bit flighty."

Dad nodded slowly, considering. "I can train her on the accounting. That's not a problem." He smiled at me. "Might be fun for you to move to London for a while. It could be a nice change of scenery for you."

I stared at him. "But...the Germans are coming."

They're mad. Both of my parents are completely mad.

"There are shelters all over the place," Mum said. "You'll be fine, dear."

She gave me one of her 'just do it so your father will stop worrying' looks and I sank down in my chair a little.

"Of course," I said quietly.

Dad beamed, giving a single nod. "Brilliant. You'll have the hobby shop doing better than ever before Christmas."

I smiled weakly.

I'm going to die in a raid, all because Cal Woodbury can't keep a bloody shop assistant.

two

CAL

"Sir, why aren't you in the war?"

My jaw tightened. It had to be the hundredth time I'd been asked that question—not since the war began, but that week.

"Well," I began, trying to come up with an excuse even a small child could understand, "I tried to join up, but they said they were full."

The boy, probably around seven or eight years old, wrinkled his nose as he considered this, his mouth forming into a tightly puckered line.

"My dad says any man not fighting in the war is a coward," said his older sister, probably around ten or eleven, her golden curls bobbing as she spoke.

I sighed. There was no use getting annoyed with children. They didn't know what they were talking about.

Their mother, her arms heavy with parcels, joined them at the shop counter. "You two, stop bothering the nice man." She sighed apologetically. "Did you both find something?"

The boy pointed at the Spitfire model airplane on the shelf behind me. "Can I get that, Mum?"

I had moved the Spitfire and Hurricane model airplanes behind the counter for safekeeping. They were one of the shop's bestselling items and were hard to come by, so I needed to make pinching them as difficult as possible. It seemed like everyone in Britain had developed an overnight love affair with everything RAF.

"Maybe for Christmas, darling. What about one of these?" Their mother pointed to a much cheaper, generic model airplane made from balsa wood. "You could paint it to look like a Spitfire."

The balsa wood airplane models were popular and inexpensive alternatives to the aluminum models. Anything made of metal was in short supply these days—anything and everything that could be melted down to make weapons and airplanes went directly to the cause.

The cause. I never thought I would be so sick of hearing two words.

The boy relented, and the trio soon filed out of the shop with their purchases.

My eyes followed them past the wide storefront windows, watching as they moved aside so another young family could pass by them on the pavement. I frowned. So many children were back in London when they were supposed to be safe in the country. It had to be difficult for the families to be parted, but everyone knew the bombing raids could happen at any moment. Airfields and anti-aircraft guns had already been targeted by the Nazis earlier that month and yet some parents chose to bring their evacuated children back to London anyway. I didn't understand it.

I pulled my ledger back out from under my desk, taking advantage of the empty shop to work on overdue paperwork. I was behind on inventory orders as well which meant yet *another* late night spent in the little office behind the shop. I also needed to find time at some point to submit another ad to the newspaper for a shop assistant. And after that was done, then maybe—just maybe—I could find time to actually go food shopping.

Pulling the pencil from behind my ear, I studied the last entry in the ledger, squinting.

Is that a seven or a one?

The bell above the door jingled, and I smiled broadly. "Good morning. Let me know if I can help you find anything."

The older chap nodded to me and went straight for the photography equipment. His skin was reddened by the August heat and his forehead had a sheen of perspiration across it. He was one of the regulars at the hobby shop and he never browsed for long, always heading directly for the photography stock.

He brought a film roll to the counter and I slid the ledger out of the way.

"How is your day going, sir?" I punched some keys into the register.

"Oh, not bad. Just enjoying the sunshine." He cleared his throat and winced slightly.

"Is there anything else you were looking for, sir?"

He puffed his chest out a little. "I was wondering why a fit young lad like you isn't in uniform."

Just before five o'clock I pulled the ladder from the back office and hauled the blackout curtains from under the front counter. They weren't technically black but a dark mossy green. They did the trick though, even satisfying the local ARP wardens who were sticklers for the blackout rules. As I went through my daily ritual of tacking the curtains over the shopfront windows, along the top and sides specifically, I stretched to reach the top corner of the curtain to stick it in place. Suddenly, the ladder shifted underneath me, tilting on one leg before falling sideways and smashing to the floor, me along with it.

The bell over the door sounded and I felt the nudge of the door push against my arm.

"Goodness!" someone said from the other side of the door, only able to open it about an inch or so.

"I'm fine," I said, pushing the ladder off, kicking the useless thing out of the way and then getting to my feet.

With me out of the way, a messenger opened the door further and poked his head in. "You're sure you're not hurt, mister?"

"Only my pride," I said, ignoring the ache spreading in my shoulder. I opened the door wider for him. "Can I help you?"

He pulled a card from his bag. "Telegram for you." He tipped his hat at me and continued on his route.

I raised an eyebrow at the heavy capital lettering of the telegram.

Maisie will assist at shop. -George Beckett

Rereading it I scratched the back of my neck. I realized telegrams charged by the word, but a *little* more explanation would have been appreciated.

I tucked it into my back pocket and finished tacking the blackout curtains in place. The tiny punctures from the tacks along the edges of the curtains had multiplied, forming bigger holes and rips. I let out a long sigh, frowning at the ratty looking fabric. Finding thick, dark fabric large enough to cover shopfront windows within my budget was likely impossible at this point. I glared at it and seriously considered covering the windows in a thick layer of black paint instead, rather than dealing with curtains twice a day. Not that finding black paint was easy either.

I slid the telegram out of my pocket and read it a third time as I locked the front door. I don't know what I expected to glean from reading it again but that didn't stop me from going over it a fourth and fifth time.

Shutting the lights off, I tucked it away again. I lugged the ledger to the back office and turned on the tiny desk lamp, splashing a golden glow onto the messy desktop and along the wood paneled walls. My shoulder gave a little twinge as I sat behind the desk, pulled the telegram out again and carefully placed it at the base of the lamp, drumming my fingertips on the open ledger page.

Roy must have told his dad I was struggling at the shop by myself, that much was clear. He must have told him about all the shop employees who had been called up for war duty or who quit on me because factory jobs paid more. It was true—I *had* been struggling to keep the shop going by myself since Roy enlisted in the Navy. He was thrilled to go to war and I was happy for him. I just figured we'd find someone else to take his place while he was away and that would be that but keeping a second employee hadn't come easily.

Maisie is coming to work at the shop with me.

Rubbing the corners of my eyes, I wondered if Roy's sister had volunteered or if George, Roy's father, asked her to do it. At least

Maisie had plenty of retail experience—she'd worked at her dad's various shops for years. I thought I remembered Roy telling me she was even managing the Hazeldon village shop.

I hadn't seen Maisie since we were kids. My most significant memory of her was from before Mum and I left Hazeldon to live in London with my uncle and his family.

I was seven or eight when I saw her running alone into the little wooded area outside the village and I followed her. She was sitting astride on a moss-covered log when I found her, taking photographs of a frog or something. Her long braids trailed down her back and her shoes were caked in mud. I sneaked up behind her and scared her and she got cross with me because the frog got away. We sat together on the log for a while and I don't know why I did it, but I asked if I could kiss her. We both leaned in, closed our eyes, our lips puckered, and we shared our first kiss together. I remembered feeling very shy around her after that.

My eyes drifted up to the little office window draped in dark green fabric. On a normal day, and depending on the time, sun crept in between the tall buildings surrounding the shop and landed on the stained glass window just right, sending a stream of emerald or ruby light cascading into the office.

But not that day though. We were certainly not living in normal times.

I sighed and cursed under my breath again. I didn't want Maisie coming to London for my sake, not when the Luftwaffe was on our doorstep.

three

Maisie

In late August I took the morning train from Hazeldon to London, gripping the worn strap of my handbag a little tighter every time the lights flickered, my gas mask bag on the seat beside me. I had only made the journey to London by myself a few times before but never since that fateful day when Mr. Chamberlain announced we were at war.

And now all I could think about as I scanned the other passengers was that no young men were among them. It was all women—varied in age—and older men.

One of those older men smoked a pipe on the seat across from me while reading a newspaper. Every front-page headline screamed about the war in enormous letters, but I had to assume the actual story content would be lacking in detail. Dad told me the newspapers had been censored terribly so Nazis could only learn what the British government wanted them to know, or information they would already have. Between that and the feel-good stories the government was forcing newspapers to publish to keep up morale, I could only guess at how challenging it was to be a wartime journalist.

The train pulled into Charing Cross and I made my way through the busy stream of passengers. I spotted three young men in Royal Navy uniforms checking the timetable and for a split second I was certain Roy was among them. My breath caught. My mouth began to form around his name, but the young man glanced my way just in time and I stopped myself from calling out to him. I quickly looked away and continued my walk.

It was only then that I noticed less than half of the people walking around the train station were carrying gas masks with them. I reached the pavement and gave a silent, cursory survey of nearby pedestrians.

Have Londoners forgotten the Germans might be coming for them?

As if on cue a lone plane buzzed overhead, and my heart thumped hard against my chest. My chocolate curls bounced against my cheeks as I looked left and right to see if anyone else was panicking. Only one person stopped to squint up at the plane for a moment before carrying on.

I took a deep breath, exhaled, and started my walk to the hobby shop. If I was to be a London resident soon, I would need to start acting like one.

I made quick work of my walk from Charing Cross to Covent Garden, trying not to focus on—or trip over—the banks of sandbags heaped against so many walls and corners. As usual Covent Garden was loud with activity. Grocery delivery boys maneuvered their high carts through crowded streets. Automobile drivers honked impatiently. Women queued up at a nearby butcher's shop, clutching their ration books for dear life. Wide shop displays showcased the newest fashions behind windows crisscrossed with Sellotape stuck in place to stop shards of glass from flying inside during a raid. I cringed, imagining pieces of glass slicing through the helpless window mannequins.

It had been a few years since I'd last seen the short but well-maintained Barnaby Street. Lined on both sides by tall Georgian style buildings and accented with bountiful flower boxes at nearly every window, it was my favorite street in London.

I stopped in front of Beckett Hobbies & More, tucked neatly in between a shoe store and a chemist shop, and grimaced at the sign above the door and windows. The paint was chipped and flaked.

That certainly won't do at all.

I began making a mental list right on the spot—but I didn't get very far with it as I noticed the windows right away. The blackout curtains were still up, and the *Closed* sign was hanging in the door even though it was nearly eleven o'clock. If Cal had changed the store hours, nobody told me.

I gave my cardigan a little tug and took a long glance down the street. No sign of him. I crossed my arms over my chest. My gaze landed on the bakery across the street. Perhaps, I thought, if Cal didn't show up I would get something to eat and then walk around London while I waited for the next train back to Hazeldon. I certainly wasn't about to stand there in front of the shop all day and wait for him. I was there to help *him* after all. I had given up managing the village shop to appease Dad and Cal couldn't even be bothered to show up on time. This new professional partnership was off to a rocky start.

The bakery door swung open and a rather good-looking young man emerged, one arm cradling a paper bag. He spotted me and jogged across the street to where I stood in front of the shop door.

"Apologies, ma'am. I didn't mean to keep you waiting," he said, fishing his keys from his pocket without meeting my gaze. "That bloody siren went half the night." He trailed off and opened the door. "Sorry," he added quickly, mumbling.

Realizing it was Cal, I opened my mouth to speak but then shut it again. I silently followed him into the shop and pretended to browse, watching him between the shelves as he hastily turned lights on, pulled the tacked-up blackout curtains down and ran his hand through his short, slightly unkempt caramel brown hair. Dark circles lined his bright blue eyes and, going by the dark stubble on his jaw, cheeks, and neck, it was clear he hadn't shaved that morning. Although filled out nicely by an athletic build, his shirt was creased with noticeable wrinkles.

He glanced up and our eyes met.

"Can I help you find something, ma'am?" His voice was low and rusty around the edges, like he just woke up from a deep sleep.

I bit my lower lip to stop myself from smirking. He really didn't recognize me at all.

"Yes, in fact, I think you can." I came out from behind a shelf. "I'm looking for a job."

He blinked slowly, processing, and straightened his posture as I approached the front counter. "If you leave your résumé with me, I'll have—" He stopped very suddenly, his eyes widening and his brow creasing. He tilted his head slightly, like a dog does when it's confused by an unusual noise. "Maisie?"

"Nice to see you again, Cal. It's been ages."

"It has, yeah." Cal rubbed the back of his neck and hesitated. "I take it your father didn't receive my letter."

"Not that I know of. What letter?"

"Well, I, um, wrote your father to tell him I did not think it wise for you to come to London," he said. "The Germans could get here any day. It's not safe."

I raised an eyebrow at him. "If it's not safe, why are you still here?"

"I can't abandon my shop."

"Well, fact is, I've already abandoned mine so I could come work here." I adjusted my bag strap on my shoulder. "It would appear you have no choice but to let me help you."

He crossed his arms over his chest. "I don't need help. I'm sorry you gave up your job already and traveled all the way to London just to hear this news but I'm fine, really."

"You told my brother otherwise."

Cal's mouth tightened. I had a sneaking suspicion that was meant to be kept between the two of them.

"If I hadn't come to help you out, my father would have, and I would rather he not be in London when the Nazis arrive." I put up a finger before he could reply. "Before you say, 'I would have told him the same thing,' don't bother. He would have persuaded you into letting him work at the store. He's very sly that way."

Cal snickered and tried to hide his tiny, knowing smile. It was the same little shy grin he had when he was a boy. I had thought I'd never see that smile again but there it was. I wondered how much he had changed since the innocent days of our childhood.

"I'm surprised your parents would want you here. In London, I mean," he added.

"Oh, I don't think Mum does. She just wants Dad here less. She knows he would be here if I didn't come. Dad knows I'll be careful—"

The front door swung open and the little bell above the door chimed as a woman entered, a large piece of card in her hand. She was likely in her fifties but dressed like someone much older, her gray hair pulled into a tight bun and adorned with a very plain, black pillbox hat. She reminded me of Miss Gulch from *The Wizard of Oz*. Scanning me up and down, her eyes narrowed slightly before she approached the counter to speak to Cal.

"Mr. Woodbury, would you mind if I put this in your window? One of my tenants just left so I need to find another one." She shoved the card at him.

"As luck would have it, I'm looking for a room to rent," I cut in. "Is it nearby?"

Cal shot me a warning look, but I ignored him.

The lady scowled at me over her rigid shoulder. "Upstairs. Are you married?"

"No."

She sniffed. "Do you have a job?"

I raised an eyebrow at Cal.

"Yes," Cal finally said with a sigh. "She starts here next week."

I gave Cal a quick smile before looking back at the woman. "Would I be able to see the room today?" I added.

"This is George Beckett's daughter, Maisie," Cal said. "Maisie, this is Mrs. Martin, our upstairs neighbor."

The words were barely out of Cal's mouth when her face softened slightly. "Heavens. I had no idea. Of course you can see the room. Come with me."

I fought the urge to roll my eyes. Older ladies adored my father. They found him charming and, I suppose, a handsome sort. Mrs. Martin was obviously another admiring fan.

Following her out of the shop, she led me to another door at the edge of the building. She unlocked it, and I followed her up the staircase within it.

"Meals are provided with rent so I'll need your ration book," she rhymed off as we climbed the stairs. "If you aren't going to be home for meals, let me know as soon as possible so no food gets wasted. People who waste food during a war should be sent to jail, that's what I say." She barely stopped for a breath before continuing. "No male visitors unless they're family. No parties, no loud music, no pets, no smoking inside and no visitors after eight o'clock. No going over the water line in the bathtub. I don't have a telephone but there is one at the end of the street that works just fine. My son installed an Anderson shelter in the back yard. If you wish to use it, get to it as soon as the air siren goes. Once the door is locked, it stays locked. I'm not going to risk getting blown up because you were dilly dallying during an air raid."

I swallowed. "Yes ma'am."

Biting my lip as she opened the door at the top of the stairs, I regretted asking to see the room in the first place, suddenly realizing why Cal had given me that look. Mrs. Martin gave me a quick tour of the kitchen, dining room, and living room—all clean and neat but looking a bit outdated and smelling like an old sweater.

"My husband—God rest him—had a hardware store where the hobby store is. I told your father he should have kept it a hardware store. I bet he regrets that now. What use is a hobby shop when there's a war on? No use at all, I say."

I didn't respond. What my family did with that retail space was none of her concern.

The bedroom was small and plain but good enough for my purposes. A narrow bed hugged the wall and a wardrobe and a small desk were tucked into two opposite corners. The small window provided a bit of natural light and a view of the bakery across the street and the flats above it. Not that I would make much use of the window—the blackout curtains would be drawn while I was home most of the time anyway.

Looking over my shoulder, I plastered on my most friendly smile. "I'll take it if you'll have me."

I handed over my first month's rent and went back to the shop.

Several customers milled about while Cal busied himself with his ledger. Leaning against the front of the counter, I fought the urge to scowl—I *never* did book work in front of customers.

Cal shook his head at me. "Mrs. Martin is a battle-axe. I can't even imagine living with her."

I shrugged. "A good portion of my customers back at the village shop are ladies like Mrs. Martin. I can handle her." My eyes landed on the bare shelves in front of the front windows. "You really ought to make use of that space."

Cal didn't even glance up. "I used to before the blackout began."

I waited for him to add context but was given none.

"*And?*"

He shot me a glare. "I ended up having to move everything off and on the shelf every time I put the curtains up and every time I had to take the curtains down. I don't have time to poke about with that." He waved his hand dismissively.

I added another item to my mental list.

"I couldn't help but notice you keep the cheaper art supply kits on the top," I said, gesturing to the shelves.

Cal sighed again and put down his pencil. "Because I would obviously rather sell the nicer, more expensive brushes and paint than the cheap kits." His jaw was clenched as he spoke. "But I'm guessing you're going to tell me to move things around."

"I was going to suggest moving the small cheaper kits to the second shelf from the bottom, around the eye height for a child." I looked at him over my shoulder. "Those kits mostly get purchased for children, right?"

Cal's eyes narrowed, darting towards the shelf and then back to me. He picked up his pencil again. "Children aren't even supposed to *be* in the city anymore."

Within seconds, a mother and her young son walked into the shop together. I slowly turned to meet Cal's glare. I beamed at him.

He looked back down at his ledger. "Don't you have a train back to Hazeldon?"

four

CAL

I will be at the shop before nine o'clock or die trying.

I knew if I arrived even a few minutes late on Maisie's first day at the shop, I'd be met with the same condescending smirk she'd had on her face when she came by the week before. I wasn't having it.

On an average Tuesday I would grab breakfast from the bakery across the street and then open the shop maybe ten or fifteen minutes after nine, but if I wanted to avoid Maisie's knowing glances I would have to arrive earlier than that.

I buttoned my yellow shirt and shoved the excess into my trousers before grabbing my belt off the bedroom floor. Catching my reflection in the mirror I wrinkled my nose, quickly unbuttoned my shirt, and tossed it on the bed. I instead grabbed a blue shirt from my wardrobe and slid my arms into the sleeves.

Earlier that morning I'd nicked myself shaving *and* managed to miss a spot on my jawline—bloody brilliant start to the day. But I still had plenty of time before I started work for the day.

Satisfied with my promptness, I strolled the short walk from my flat in Holborn—weaving in between wig-wearing barristers sporting robes and grim expressions—to nearby Covent Garden with its busy vegetable stalls, flower sellers, and wide range of shops.

George Beckett was lucky to get the shop for the price he did. I could only assume Mrs. Martin gave him a good price because she fancied him and didn't know how much the property was actually worth.

My pleasant walk ended abruptly when I rounded the corner onto Barnaby Street. My shoulders fell as I spotted Maisie standing by the door, her small hands folded neatly in front of her, the strap of her gas mask bag hanging over one arm. Cursing under my breath, I wondered how long she'd been standing there.

"You're early," I mumbled as I stuck my key in the door.

"And good morning to you too," she said, her silvery voice sounding far too jolly for that time of day.

"We open at nine o'clock so there is really no reason to be here so early." I opened the door and gave a 'ladies first' gesture with my hand.

"Oh, I know. I like to be able to take my time getting things ready for the day," she explained. "Oh, that reminds me. I had an idea for the blackout curtains."

"What about—what are you doing?"

Before I could finish my sentence, she slid her shoes off and hopped up on the display window ledge to untack the dark green curtains.

"Here, take these," she said, dropping the tacks into my palm.

As she stretched to reach the tacks at the top of the window, she stood on tiptoe, her feet arching.

Her feet are so small.

My eyes followed the dark line of her stockings up the back of her shapely calves and up the rest of her curvaceous frame. With her arms up above her head, reaching for the tacks keeping the curtains up, half an inch of milk white midriff was left bare between the top of her black knee-length skirt and the bottom edge of her floral print blouse.

I pulled my eyes away as a few more tacks were dropped into my palm. Fighting the urge to look back at the soft pale skin directly in my line of sight, I searched my mind frantically for something to say.

Maisie spoke up first, slinging the dark green curtain over her arm. "Why aren't you in uniform anyway? I was surprised when you didn't sign up with Roy."

Before I could offer my hand to help her down from the window display, she jumped off and slid her delicate feet back into her shoes.

"I was going to," I said, depositing the tacks into the pencil cup on the front counter. "They couldn't promise me my own tank so I declined their invitation."

She smiled. "Indeed." She pulled a little sewing kit from her skirt pocket, slid onto the stool behind the counter and went to work altering something along the edge of the curtain fabric.

"It's probably for the best," I added, lifting the inventory clipboard from its hook behind the counter and grabbing a pencil. "They said my good looks would be a distraction for everyone fighting. 'He's a danger to us all,' they said."

Maisie let out a little giggle. "Naturally."

As she smiled, dimples blossomed just below the apples of her cheeks. Very suddenly and without warning, the snow white skin of her midriff appeared in my mind. Fortunately the ring of the bell above the door startled me from my trance.

The older gentleman—one of my regulars—nodded to us as he entered and headed for the stamp and coin collecting supplies.

"Good morning, sir," Maisie said, once again speaking up before I could. "Let us know if we can help you find anything."

I busied myself checking our supplies on another shelf at the back of the store. A moment later, Maisie's voice caught my attention.

Peering around a shelf of woodworking tools, I glared at the back of her head as she needlessly pestered the customer. In my experience men usually disliked being asked questions while they shopped. Men almost always knew what they were looking for and if they couldn't find it, they left. Simple as that.

I couldn't quite hear their interaction but within a minute, Maisie was ringing up the man's purchase. I expected her to call me over to help her, but the call never came. The doorbell chimed and the man was on his way.

"Congratulations," I said, returning to the counter. "Your first sale."

She flashed that smug grin of hers and I felt my back go rigid.

"He was looking for an album for stamps but I knew we didn't have the kind he was looking for."

I nodded. "Stamp collectors are very particular about their albums."

Maisie gave a little shrug. "I recommended a different one and mentioned what a great hobby stamp collecting would be for evenings in the Anderson shelter and he ended up getting two of the albums I suggested." The self-satisfied expression on her face stayed put. "Oh, and a magnifying glass."

Blinking at her for a moment, I felt the heat raise in my neck. I gave a single nod and returned to the woodworking shelf.

My grip on my pencil tightened and the pencil marks in my inventory sheet suddenly became a lot darker and deeper than they had been minutes before.

That afternoon a young woman came into the shop, barely acknowledged either of us, and rushed to the back shelf like a mouse fleeing to its hole in the wall. Maisie and I exchanged confused glances.

Maisie checked on her while I busied myself with a product catalog. So many items made from metal were now impossible to get so I had to get creative with replacement products. More and more often, I wrote to the distributors for products and they responded with short apologies about having nothing available for me. I could only sell so many balsa wood model airplanes before the shop shut down.

Not that taking on a second employee would help financial matters much.

My new colleague returned to the counter with a shrug.

"Just browsing," she whispered.

When the unusual customer didn't show herself again, I picked up my clipboard and pretended to be inventorying dollhouse building materials and the tiny furniture we sold to go in them.

It was then that I felt her eyes on me.

I slowly lifted my head to meet her gaze through a supply shelf and she immediately looked away.

"Miss, are you sure I can't—"

"No, that's alright. Thank you," she blurted as she rushed down the aisle and to the exit. “Sorry,” she added before whipping the door shut behind her.

“What on earth?” Maisie said. “Did she nick something?”

I gave a quick scan of all the shelves near the back of the store. If she *had* stolen something, I didn’t know what it was.

“Nothing is missing,” I said.

“Maybe she wanted to spy on you,” she added, bemusement in her voice.

“Oh, I’m being targeted by the Nazis now, am I?”

“No, I meant she fancies you.” Maisie laughed. “Why would the Germans spy on you?”

I poked my head out from around a shelf and glared at her.

“By the way,” she added, “why aren’t you fighting the Germans?”

I leaned against a shelf and took a long look at her. “You really want to know?”

She nodded slowly, her expression turning serious.

“I suppose you should know anyway.” I let out a long breath and looked directly at her. “I’m secretly a dog in a man costume.”

five

Maisie

It was unseasonably warm that Saturday, even early in the morning.

If I had still been back in Hazeldon, I would have been counting the minutes until I could close up shop and escape to the forest grotto only I knew about. I would don my swimming costume and cap and sit on a rock or dip my feet into the fresh, cool water and listen to the river washing over the rocks and trickling down into surrounding currents.

Instead of my private forest oasis I was in London, doing something I knew I was not supposed to do.

Although the store had a steady stream of customers, Cal's expression went grave each time he worked at his ledger. I knew he would never willingly show me his books or ask for my help if the store was in financial trouble. But this wasn't just about the shop. If I was on a fool's errand of trying to aid a failing business beyond help, I needed to know.

It was only around six o'clock so Mrs. Martin and her other tenant, Nora, were still asleep when I left the flat and opened the shop using the key Cal gave me the day before. Locking the door behind me, I went to the little office at the back of the shop and stuck the key into the lock, not even sure if it would work. I let out a breath when the key turned smoothly and let myself in and turned on the desk lamp.

I should not be doing this.

His tiny desk was littered with receipts and reminders and torn out pages from product catalogs. An empty teacup with a ring of brown tea in the bottom sat at the corner. Since the office was more of a closet than a room, I didn't have far to look to find the ledger. I flipped open to a recent page and studied the numbers, squinting hard to decipher Cal's narrow, cramped handwriting.

Sighing, I pulled one of the old ledgers off the nearby shelf and compared the numbers from a past date. Recognizing my brother's handwriting instantly, I knew the second ledger would have been from before the war started. Before city dwellers fled the city in droves. Before food and material rationing began. Before children were shoved onto trains and sent to some unknown location in the country to live with strangers.

Not that all of those children had actually stayed in the country like they were supposed to. And just because some of the evacuees returned to London didn't mean people suddenly had money for luxury items like hobby supplies.

Comparing the numbers in the two ledgers made several things clear to me; the number of sales were still reasonably good despite everything, but the costs of products had gone up dramatically.

I winced, realizing my wages were an extra drain on shop resources the shop couldn't realistically handle. I closed the ledgers and put them back where I found them. I turned off the light, locked everything up again, and climbed the stairs back up to the flat, all the while the same six words running through my head over and over.

What am I going to do?

I found Mrs. Martin eating breakfast. She pursed her lips and eyed me as I sat down.

"You're up early," she said. "Nora likes to sleep in on weekends. I can't sleep in. It gives me a headache."

I nodded and poured myself some tea. In the week I lived with Mrs. Martin, I learned a great many things gave Mrs. Martin headaches, including but not limited to the wireless being played too loudly, the voices of most BBC presenters, children, automobiles outside, telephones ringing (which is why she didn't have a phone in the flat), food with too many different spices, dealing with ration books, and the smell of perfume. The only thing she actually did seem to approve of was the royal family.

"I heard they're going to ration tea," Mrs. Martin said, shaking her head. "Imagine. The people would revolt, that's what I say."

I should just go home to Hazeldon.

By coming to London and forcing my help upon Cal, I put the shop in a worse position than it was to begin with. I'd given up a good job for this. At least when I was in Hazeldon, I was with my parents and not paying to live with a woman who said nothing unless it was a complaint.

Cal could have told me he couldn't afford a second employee, but by the sounds of it he couldn't handle the shop on his own either way.

We need to bring in more money. That's all there is to it.

"Miss Beckett, are you even listening to me?"

"Apologies," I muttered. "I was just thinking about, uh, the King and Queen."

Mrs. Martin gave a short nod of approval. "Mm."

I opened the shop again about ten minutes before nine, beginning the day by taking the blackout curtain down from the front windows. It was much easier now thanks to the string loops I'd added, and the tacks kept in place in the wall. With the curtains down, morning sun poured in through the wide front windows, filling the two rows of shelves with light. The well-worn floors could have used a polish, the paint outside a refresh, and a few buttons on the register were finicky but it was cozy and homey. Cal and Roy hadn't changed much when they took it over so many of my father's personal touches were still visible throughout the shop. Shelving and signage painted in a different color depending on what type of product was displayed there, the model airplanes hanging from the ceiling in a miniature dogfight, and the stained glass window in the office—all of those details were George

Beckett originals.

Cal arrived about fifteen minutes after nine, a scone in hand. He nodded at me while taking a bite and a few crumbs landed on his chin.

"I made tea if you'd like some," I offered.

He let out sort of a quiet grunt in response and headed for the back room where the kettle and tea things were kept. I heard the jingle of his keys at his office first and the familiar creak of the door. Doing my best to seem cavalier, I leant against the doorway to the back part of the store.

"Do you recall yesterday when I was looking for some paint in the cellar to touch up the sign outside?"

He popped the remaining bite of his scone into his mouth and carried his tea to his office. "No."

"Well, I was," I said hastily. "When I was down there, I noticed the room that was going to be for photo developing. There are still developing chemicals down there and we have everything we need to offer that service."

"Did you find any?"

"Hmm?"

"Paint for the sign."

"Oh, no. But I know how to develop film. It could be an extra service we could offer to customers."

Cal slid his ledger from the shelf, exactly from where I had returned it earlier that morning and flipped to the last page. My stomach turned as my eyes quickly scanned the little room. What if I left *something* out of place and he figured out that I had been in there earlier? What if he could *sense* it?

He glanced up at me. "One of the reasons I hired you was—"

"Because I forced you into it."

"Well, yes. *That* and because I need another employee in the shop, not mucking around downstairs."

"I could attend to it between nine and ten o'clock when we're not busy anyway," I said, gesturing to the empty store behind me. "It might be a useful extra service for the shop."

'Useful extra service for the shop' was the best way I could come up with to say 'a way for us to make a little more money.'

Cal took another gulp from his teacup. "Come to think of it, a few photographer customers have been asking me if I know where they can get their film developed since the camera shop three streets over closed when the war began." His eyes narrowed as he considered. "Do you think we have everything we need, or do we need to invest in anything expensive before we put a sign in the window?"

"I can take a second look but I think everything is there, ready to go."

A pinprick of regret stabbed my heart at the words. That room had been set up for Aunt Jean and 'ready to go' for her, not me. But that's not how things turned out.

"Yes, please do have another look just in case and I'll source whatever we need."

I beamed. "So, that's a yes then? You're taking my suggestion?"

He sighed and went back to his book work. "Yes. I figure it's easier than arguing with you about it."

"And what about the paint for the sign? I don't think we need much, maybe a small—"

"The sign is fine."

"*Is* it?" I wrinkled my nose before casting a quick glance around the shop. "Actually, inside could use some new paint too."

Cal glared up at me. "Are you just about finished?"

"What do you mean?"

"I didn't hire you to come in and make a bunch of changes to the shop," he snapped. "I don't need your advice. The store is fine the way it is."

Apparently it's not fine *since the shop is hemorrhaging income every week.* I wanted to scream at him.

"I… I just want to help," I said instead.

"Well, stop helping and focus on the job you're here to do." He looked back down at his ledger. "I don't even know why you would want to work here if the shop needs as many improvements as you seem to think it does."

"I'm here because my father asked me to come," I said firmly. "This place means a lot to him and he means a lot to me. I know what

I'm doing."

"No offense but managing a village shop is a little different from managing a store in London," he mumbled, still not bothering to look at me as he spoke. "If I wanted your suggestions, I would ask for them."

"Oh, you most certainly would *not* ask," I spat, moments before a few customers came in.

Smiling, I closed the door to the back section of the shop and assisted them. Once they left, I felt my shoulders stiffen and my jaw tighten. I offered to create more income for the shop and he didn't seem the slightest bit grateful.

When he eventually emerged from the back room, we both avoided eye contact. I grabbed the clipboard off the hook and stormed to the back shelves to do inventory. I didn't want to be anywhere near that stubborn crumb if I could help it.

I was only a few minutes into doing inventory when the door chimed, and a customer headed directly for the back shelves where I was, her heels clicking hard on the floor as she walked. The brim of her cloche was pulled down so far over her eyes I couldn't tell if she saw me or not until she stopped very suddenly. She hesitated and then whipped down the aisle in front of mine and stood there for a moment.

Since I recognized her immediately as the same young woman from before, it's safe to say she was a truly terrible spy.

I went about my work while keeping an eye on her through the open shelving, just in case she decided to slip a birdwatching guidebook into her handbag and make a dash for the door.

She plucked a book off the shelf and opened to the middle of it, holding it in front of her face and peering through the gaps in the shelves to watch Cal at the counter. As she tipped the brim of her hat up a bit, a few yellow blonde curls escaped.

She stayed there, frozen, gawking at Cal over a book for several minutes. She was so focused on him she didn't even detect me watching her. She didn't even notice when I went around the corner and joined her in the same aisle.

"Excuse me," I said softly so as not to startle her. "Can I help you find something?"

She gaped at me with wide, blinking eyes. She was young, maybe eighteen or nineteen. Hesitating, she opened her mouth slightly before biting her lip and looking to the exit.

"Miss, are you alright?"

"I'm fine," she blurted. "I'm sorry. I-I-I have to go."

She tossed the book back, leaving it laying sideways on top of the row of books instead of sliding it back in the proper section, and rushed past me to the door. I leaned out of the aisle and watched her open the door and stop in the doorway.

"I'm… I'm sorry," she said before fleeing.

I hurried to the pavement to see which way she'd gone but she had already disappeared into the crowd of weekend shoppers.

Closing the door behind me, I gave Cal a questioning look. "You don't have an angry former girlfriend, do you?"

He rifled through a stack of receipt slips and didn't look up. "Not that I'm aware of."

"That's the same woman from the other day," I said. "She was staring at you. She was hiding her face behind a book, but she was *not* subtle."

"Yes, I noticed," he said. "Very strange."

"You're not concerned at all?"

"No, not particularly. We get a few weird customers in here on occasion."

"She's not a mate from school or a neighbor or something?"

"Not that I know of."

"And why aren't you in uniform?"

He didn't even look up. "Because I secretly love the Germans."

I was hanging the blackout curtain for the night when the siren began to scream.

Its wails came in waves, starting low, building to a booming crescendo and then receding before building up again, each undulation overlapping slightly with the one before it. The sound filled my ears and reverberated in my head.

Several shoppers on the other side of the window scurried for cover while others continued their normal pace. My heart thumped hard in my chest and I nearly lost my footing on the ladder when I looked over my shoulder to see Cal's response.

He shook his head. "Don't worry. We've had so many false alarms, I've lost count."

"I don't know, Cal." I lifted the curtain and peered out. "Some people seem to be taking it seriously."

"Oh, yes, that's right. You haven't heard the siren in the city yet." He shrugged. "Well, you'll soon get used to it," he added, mumbling, "I hope you don't mind having your sleep interrupted."

I thought of Mrs. Martin and her stern warnings about being late to the Anderson shelter in the back garden. As if on cue, the sound of someone rushing down the side staircase next to the shop reached my ears—I assumed it was Mrs. Martin on her way to the shelter. I wondered if Nora was still upstairs or if she was out somewhere, enjoying the sunshine.

As I was heading for the back room to grab the broom to give the shop a final sweep, the scratching sound from Cal's pencil suddenly stopped and we looked at one another. The wail of the siren stopped but it was soon followed by a very different sound altogether—a low droning hum.

Cal and I hurried outside to the street where many shoppers were all doing the exact same thing. Several other shopkeepers came out to investigate too. Someone came out of the bakery across the street, their apron white with flour and their eyes wide with fear. Before I could even look to the sky the realization hit my gut like a brick.

"Oh, God," I whispered.

Planes. Lots of them. Dotting the clear blue sky above London like a swarm of black flies. In perfect formation, they moved like a pack of wolves towards the Thames. Nothing was in their way. No anti-aircraft guns. No Hurricanes. No Spitfires. They flew straight towards their target, entirely unheeded. Not even the few massive, silver barrage balloons hovering in the sky around the city were a deterrent. They kept coming.

"Bloody hell," Cal said.

Like me, he was unable to tear his eyes away from the sight.

An ARP warden blew hard on their whistle nearby, startling us out of our trance, and shouted at us to find shelter immediately.

"Come to the Anderson shelter," I said, grabbing Cal's arm. "It's closer."

I was grateful he didn't try to argue with me. Instead, we went back into the shop and Cal stopped to lock the front door, his vibrating hands causing the keys to jingle together.

"Leave it," I ordered and grabbed his empty hand, pulling him to the back room and out the back door, snatching the strap of my gas mask on the way out.

Mrs. Martin took the government's recommendation to the British people to grow vegetables very seriously as almost every inch of the garden was now dedicated to growing food. I knew she'd have my head if we stepped on anything, so I made sure to watch my step as we dashed towards the metal dome of the Anderson shelter and pulled the door open.

Mrs. Martin was already inside when we arrived, sitting on the narrow bed that was pushed up against the left wall of the shelter. She scowled at Cal as he followed me inside.

"No, no, no. There's no room for him," she said. "He can go to a shelter—"

"Mrs. Martin," I snapped, "perhaps you aren't aware but this isn't just another false alarm. There are Nazi planes flying overhead."

She was, in fact, not aware. She blinked at me, her mouth hanging open.

"Oh my word," she said quietly, looking away from us. "Oh, my word."

Since the other half of the shelter was taken up by a bunk bed, Cal offered to take the top bunk, laying down on his back since the curved metal ceiling was too low for a person to sit upright. I took the lower bunk and tried not to watch Mrs. Martin as she closed her eyes and whispered a prayer.

A moment later Nora arrived and shut the door firmly behind her.

"This is mad. I've never seen anything like it," she said between gasps for breath, her hand on her chest. "Oh, hi Cal." She took a seat beside me on the bottom bunk and smiled weakly, her large green eyes warm and friendly. "Welcome to London, Maisie."

I snickered. "So glad I got here just in time for—"

There was a sudden loud boom. It seemed far away but it was hard to tell from within that tin can. More booms followed, but thankfully none seemed to be close to us. I felt bad for even having such a thought.

"I wonder where they're dropping bombs." Nora unbuckled her fashionable high heels and slid them under the bunk.

She scooted further back on the bed so her slender frame leaned against the corrugated steel wall, her narrow skirt making it a bit tricky to move. Everything from her strawberry blonde waves to her flawless makeup to her pristine stockings was classic London style—polished and put together. This country girl found it all a bit intimidating.

"Probably the docks," Cal said from above us. "Our imports come in through there. They want to starve us out."

I winced. Some of the poorest Londoners lived quite close to the docks, many in cramped living quarters. Their lives were about to be changed forever.

The flickering flame on Mrs. Martin's candle was the only light inside our little hole in the ground. It was such a small space. I wondered how a family with several children would deal with such an environment.

If we die in here, at least I'll die knowing how a sardine feels.

"You said your son built this shelter for you, Mrs. Martin?" She looked up when I said her name, seeming a bit startled. "Is he serving in the war?"

"Yes. He's in North Africa now." She nodded, her eyes focused on nothing in particular. Suddenly, she looked up at the top bunk. "Mr. Woodbury, why aren't you in uniform?"

Nora and I both looked at the bunk above ours, as if we could see Cal through it. I heard him exhale before he responded.

"Both of my legs are missing."

Around half six, a longer, even siren blared outside the shelter.

I looked at Nora and Mrs. Martin. "Does that mean it's safe now?"

Cal swung his legs over the upper bunk and hopped down. "Safe enough anyway." He listened at the door before letting himself out, shielding his brow as the evening sun hit his eyes.

I slid off the bed and followed him out. Naturally, the first thing he checked on was the shop. While he checked the windows and shelves, I let myself out the front door to check the street for holes in the ground or fires. Everything on Barnaby Street was intact, just eerily quiet.

"We ought to put Sellotape across the windows in case a bomb drops nearby," I said from the open doorway. "It doesn't look very nice, a big crisis-cross of tape, but I can't imagine new windows are easy to come by right now."

"Nothing is," he added. "But yes, you're right. I have some Sellotape downstairs. I'll come by tomorrow while the shop is closed and tape them up."

Relieved to hear him take my advice, I smiled at him even while he avoided eye contact with me still. His pained gaze went right from the windows to the patch of sky over my shoulder.

Smoke from distant fires smothered the sky in a blanket of ash gray. Sirens from emergency vehicles blended together, all speeding in the same direction.

"You might want to find a better way to light the Andie," he said, sounding miles away. "Candles and batteries for a torch are hard to find as it is. They're about to get even harder to find."

I nodded. "Right." It's all I could think to say.

Cal had his keys in his hand, so I moved so he could lock the front door properly.

Folding my arms around myself, I stood there. I didn't know what to do with myself. Going back to the flat was likely what I was *supposed* to do but going home after a workday felt so… mundane. So normal. That day was profoundly not normal.

"I might try to find an ARP warden and see if they know which areas are safe. I have family in Clerkenwell. Actually, I'll probably try to get over there if I can and make sure they're alright." He said this like it was nothing—like he was just going over for a quick chat or something.

"Cal, don't," I said. "They could come back."

We both knew very well who I meant by 'they.'

His jaw stiffened and he exhaled, a look of resignation about him. I nodded and started for the back door.

"You should go back to Hazeldon."

I turned around and gave him a playful smirk. "You're stuck with me—"

"I'm not joking." The hardness of his eyes confirmed that much. "This has nothing to do with the shop. London is not safe right now."

"You can't run the shop alone—"

"That should not be your concern right now," he snapped, his volume climbing. "Nazi planes just dropped bombs on London and you're worried about the *shop*. Why are you even here? It's not even *your* shop!"

"But it *should* be mine!"

The words left my throat before I could stop, the sound of them surprising even me. Cal's eyebrows went up just before I whirled around and started for the back door again. Cal caught hold of my arm before I reached it.

"Wait, Maisie, what are you even talking about?"

When I turned back around to face him again, I was looking directly at his chest. His Adam's apple bobbed as he took a step back, putting a little bit of distance between us.

"What do you mean it should be yours?"

I sighed and studied the floor. "*I'm* the one who worked in Dad's shop. Roy never cared about having a shop in his entire life. When do you recall Roy *ever* spending any time in Dad's shop because he wanted to be there or because he wanted to learn?"

Cal frowned, a crease forming between his eyebrows.

"Roy only agreed to take the hobby shop because it meant getting out of the village and living in London. You know it's true." I shook my head. "I shouldn't have said anything."

He leaned his back against the counter, taking his time to respond. "Why do you think your dad gave Roy the shop and not you?"

"You know very well why." I rolled my eyes. "Because I should be at home with babies, not behind a counter."

"Well, if it means anything, I *do* care about the shop even if Roy doesn't."

I gave a little shrug. "I know you do."

Cal slid his hands into his trouser pockets and studied me for a moment. A tiny smile formed on his mouth. "You might be insane."

I stared at him. "What?"

"There are bombs falling out of the sky and yet you are *still* determined to prove yourself to your father."

I blinked at him. "That's not-that's not what—"

"Oh, yes, it is." He laughed. "That's exactly why you're here. If that's not it, then why the hell are you here?"

I opened my mouth to speak. Nothing came out.

Cal sighed. "Don't make me fire you, Maisie."

I straightened. "You are *not* firing me. I am *not* going back to Hazeldon. You need me." I shrugged again. "There are eight million people in London. We can't all flee to the country. Some of us need to stick it out and—" I glanced at a nearby shelf. "—sell paint brushes." I pulled the strap of my gas mask bag higher up on my shoulder and turned on my heel. "Assuming we don't get bombed before then, see you on Tuesday."

The siren screeched again that evening at half past eight. Mrs. Martin, Nora and I returned to the Anderson shelter, this time bringing blankets and pillows with us. Nora even brought a deck of cards with her and we played a few games, squinting at our cards in the dark, as the drones of the planes roared overhead once more.

"I hope Cal didn't end up walking to Clerkenwell," I thought out loud as Nora tucked the cards away.

I glanced at Mrs. Martin in the bunk mere inches from ours, somehow snoring away, despite our hushed conversation and the repeated hollow booming sounds off in the distance.

"Mrs. Martin mentioned you and Cal knew one another from before you started working at the shop," Nora said, posing it as a question. "She said your brother co-owns the shop?"

"Cal and my brother have been best friends since they were four.

I was only the annoying sister," I said. "My brother doesn't know this but Cal was actually my first kiss."

The faint glimmer of the candlelight highlighted the look of absolute delight on Nora's face and I immediately regretted sharing that detail.

"Oh, my goodness," she whispered. "That is so adorable."

If Mrs. Martin wasn't sleeping nearby, I think Nora likely would have squealed with joy.

"He's very handsome," she added with a wide grin.

I shrugged. "I suppose he is."

six

Cal

The night of the first raid was a long one.

After a quick dinner at the flat, I pushed my dishes aside and flipped open my ledger to catch up on some paperwork. My ledger almost always came home with me as there never seemed to be enough time in the day to handle everything.

Until that day.

After a moment of checking the numbers and the stack of receipts I'd tucked inside earlier that day, I realized I was… I was caught up. I'd finished contacting my distributors so that was taken care of too.

Puzzled, I closed the ledger and drummed my fingers on the smooth cover. I hadn't been without paperwork to do since, well, since the day Roy and I unlocked the front door and called the shop our own.

I scratched the back of my neck and looked around my silent flat. Dragging myself to the kitchen sink, I pulled the window curtain open only an inch. The thick, rolling towers of smoke from the East End fires had begun to fade into the darkening sky. I regretted not going to Clerkenwell to check on my family like I intended. Maisie had worried needlessly—I would have been fine. Like a fool and a coward, I went right home.

I let the curtain fall closed again and headed for my bedroom, grabbing my copy of *The Hobbit* off the bedside table before my head landed on the pillow.

Only moments later I heard someone come into my flat. I looked up to see Maisie peering around the doorframe at me, the gold flecks of her brown eyes flashing as she came toward me. Her tight black dress hugged her body, showcasing the wondrous curve of her narrow waist and wide hips.

"What are you doing here?" I sat up.

She didn't answer me. She smiled and slid herself between my knees. Bending over, she took my face in her hands before bringing her mouth to mine and laying the smallest, most tender kiss onto my bottom lip. She laid a second kiss on my cheek and then another higher up on my jaw.

When her red lips found my ear, she whispered, "You need to go."

"Where? Why?"

She stood again. "Go, Cal. Go."

The air raid siren wailed and I jolted upright in bed, a stream of drool clinging to the right side of my mouth. I wiped at it and picked my book off the floor, my eyes lingering on the empty dark space where Dream Maisie had stood. Feeling an uncomfortable tightness in my trousers, I swore and grabbed a rumpled knit jumper from a chair in the living room before dashing out the door, nearly forgetting to grab my keys on the way out.

My neighbors and I nodded politely to one another, all of us walking quickly but not running, just as the government advised. It couldn't have been very late as most of them were still in their daytime clothes. Or maybe they all expected a second air raid that night and decided not to risk having to go out in their pajamas. Only little Diana from the end of the hall—about four or five years old—was in her nightgown. Her mother carried her down the stairs while Diana had her tiny arms wrapped around a well-loved teddy bear. Diana clamped her free hand over her ear, shielding it from the whining moans of the siren.

A few of our neighbors opted to shelter in the cellar of our building. Knowing the ineptitude of my landlord, I chose to take my chances on the nearest public shelter instead and it looked as if most of my neighbors were of the same mind about it.

Once out on the street, we followed the sound of the ARP warden's whistle and the stream of other locals, all heading to the shelter. The street was so dark with the blackout I had no way of knowing how many others were there with me. I kept my eyes on the pavement edge where city officials added white paint to help pedestrians, motorists, and cyclists find their way in the pitch-black night.

"Everyone, please, quickly," the ARP warden shouted, "into the shelter. Thank you, this way. Please don't run. Into the shelter everyone, thank you." He waved and pointed, waved and pointed.

I recognized his nasally voice right away; he was the warden who barked at me in the early days of the blackout for accidentally leaving my kitchen curtain open. I suppose he was only doing his job, but he didn't have to be such a prat about it.

My neighbors and I reached the small structure on the next street over. I could hear little Diana asking her mother when she could go back to bed. Poor thing.

I strolled by the shelter every morning on my way to work and didn't expect much from it. It looked shoddily built, a bit small, and quite dark.

What I found once inside was even more disappointing.

My eyes adjusted to the dark a little by then. Sandbags were heaped on top of it and along the sides of it. The entrance was a simple wooden door frame—one almost felt like a cow being herded into a barn. Inside, the only place to sit inside were two long benches up against the walls. Naturally all seats were taken by the time our lot arrived. A few people brought their gas masks with them; most hadn't. I'd forgotten mine.

If I lived a bit closer to Covent Garden I would have found myself banging on the door of Mrs. Martin's Anderson shelter, begging to be let in. By comparison the Andie was cozy and private. And Maisie was there.

The only light inside was from a quivering candle on the far end of the shelter, casting eerie shapes onto the brick walls. Seeing a few others sit in place, I decided to do the same.

Quiet chatter filled the shelter for a few minutes. Once the boom-boom-boom of the bombs began, the shelter went quiet.

Diana and her mother were seated on the floor nearby, the little girl sniffling into her mother's shoulder. She looked at me with watery eyes and I forced a comforting smile. She buried her face into her mother's hair and sobbed.

Hell isn't being hit by a bomb. Hell is waiting to be hit by a bomb, surrounded by strangers, in a poorly built brick shack that doesn't have a toilet.

The all clear siren sounded at half past four the following morning. I stumbled home in a fog and slept most of the day.

Unfortunately, the Luftwaffe returned to London the following night. And the night after that. And the night after that.

After the first night there, I swore I'd never return to that godforsaken shelter and decided to take my chances with the basement of my building. Each night I took a pillow and a blanket downstairs and stuffed my ears with candle wax to block out the sound of the bombs. It muffled the sounds, if the bombs were far enough away. However, every time a bomb landed within a few miles of Holborn the building shook, and unsettled dust sprang out from cracks in the foundation.

Diana's mother joined me in the basement a week after the raids began, her little blonde daughter noticeably absent.

"Where's your girl?"

She smiled weakly, her eyes empty. "I sent her to live with my aunt in the country." She sighed and adjusted her pillow. "I should have kept her there in the first place."

The Germans returned to London every night. Every morning, sleep-deprived city dwellers emerged from their shelters, pillows under their arms and dark shadows under their eyes, and ambled home to get ready for their workday. We carried on during the day like nothing was happening.

Being late because a bus had to navigate around a bomb crater in the street became an everyday occurrence. The East End, particularly homes and businesses near the Thames, were pummeled worse than any of us but all of London was peppered with gaping pits where bombs landed. Some streets looked perfectly untouched by the madness, except for one structure in the middle that looked like some cruel older brother had taken a cricket bat to his sister's dollhouse.

Days turned into weeks. It immediately became apparent the city's raid preparations were not sufficient for the needs of its residents, so Londoners soon took their safety into their own hands and forced their way into underground stations all over the city. Even before the nightly siren went, families, friends, and neighbors were already down in their subterranean cities.

In the moments when I managed to block out the sounds of sirens, explosions, and the eerie whistling the bombs made as they fell from the sky, I was actually able to sleep a little. Exhaustion can only last so long before sleep pushes its way in, no matter the time of day. Some days Maisie and I took turns having naps in the office while the other managed the shop. Those few minutes of rest were vital for my sanity.

Customers continued to visit the shop, somehow. Many looked for activities they could do in a shelter. In those hours when Maisie and I were both on the shop floor, I tried not to look at her for too long. I figured if we happened to make eye contact, she would be able to tell what the two of us did in my dreams nearly every night.

One day in mid-September I was doing inventory and Maisie was writing to our suppliers. I was so focused on what I was doing that I almost missed my spy entering the shop.

I nudged Maisie and nodded to the door while I headed to the shelves, inching closer to the mysterious young woman. Maisie moved to the door, just in case she made a run for it.

"Miss, can I help you with something?"

She let out a little gasp. "No, I'm fine. I-I-I shouldn't have come." Her eyes darted to the door and she looked back at me, panicked. She was like a frightened rabbit, eyes wide and dark.

"My apologies, miss," I said, making sure to keep my tone as gentle as possible. "Do I know you? You've been in here several times—"

"I'm sorry." She bit her lip. "But...you *are* Paul Woodbury's son, aren't you?"

I quirked an eyebrow. "Yes?"

She hesitated.

"Is...is he alright?"

"Yes, he's fine," she replied quickly. "I wanted to meet you because..." She winced. "He's my father too."

The realization came hard and fast, like a slap in the face. At a loss of what else to do, I stared at her. Maisie appeared at my side, looking up at me, her soft brown eyes full of concern.

"Why don't the two of you go now and grab some food and talk?" It wasn't so much a suggestion as a softly spoken order.

I nodded again and looked at the young woman over my shoulder, now out from her hiding place among the shelves. "Let's go to the pub."

On the next street over was my local pub of choice, The Ox and Crane, a hole in the wall with wooden booths, a dart board, and cold beer. I ordered some chips although I had never felt less hungry in my life.

"I'm sorry," I said, shaking my head, "I didn't even ask your name."

She smiled shyly. "Susan."

"And your mother is Ada?"

She nodded.

"And how old are you?"

She cast her gaze to the window at the front of the pub.

I grimaced and laughed at myself. "I'm sorry. I'm in shock. I know you're not supposed to ask a lady that—"

"It's not that. I would have lots of questions too. I know *I* did when I learned *you* existed," she said, looking back at me. "I'm almost twenty-one."

I swallowed. "That's impossible."

I was twenty-one.

"That's what I said when I found out when you were born." She lit a cigarette and took a long, nervous drag. "I only found out about all of this about six months ago."

I ran a hand through my hair. "Do I have any other siblings I don't know about?"

"I have two younger brothers. Well, *we* do. Harry is eighteen, Glenn is fifteen."

My gut ached. It was all too much. I took a few deep breaths to steady my shaking hands, hiding them under the table.

"You didn't know our father wasn't married to your mum when you were born?"

My father had begged Mum for a divorce after he moved out, but it took a few years for her to finally give in—to finally realize he wasn't coming back.

"I only found out because I happened to find their wedding certificate and I noticed the year on it was wrong," she said, brushing some yellow-blonde hair away from her face. "I actually believed it was a mistake on the certificate. It didn't even occur to me they would lie to me. I confronted them, and they came clean about the existence of Dad's family before us."

"Before." More like 'during' by the sounds of it.

The server brought our chips, but I don't think either of us touched our food. My blood pulsed in my ears, nearly drowning out the chatter of the other pub patrons and the low music coming from the wireless.

"Just to clarify, my dad—sorry, *our* dad—and your mother were together for years before he…left," I said, struggling to find the right words. "You must have thought it strange he was not at home very much when you and your brothers were children and then suddenly, he was always there?"

"We were told he got a new job and would have a lot more time for us."

I sat back in my seat and exhaled slowly. "And a lot less time for me."

Dad had all but disappeared from my life when he left us. I got the occasional letter on my birthday and I saw him in London only a few times growing up. Of course, he never took me to his home and now I understood why.

"Do you know if my mum knows about you and our brothers?"

"She knows about me, but I don't think she knows about them."

Mum knew I had a sister and never told me.

"Does Dad know you found me?"

"Yes." Susan tapped her cigarette into the ashtray. "He wants to see you and he wants you to meet Harry and Glenn." She paused before sharing a tiny smile. "You look so much like them."

That sentiment turned my stomach. My neck felt hot and my mouth tasted bitter. The air in the room felt tighter. I slid from the booth and threw some money on the table.

"I have to go. Please don't come to the shop again." I headed for the door.

"Wait," she called to me, "at least take our address—"

"I don't want it." I shoved the pub door open and escaped onto the pavement, gulping oxygen like a shipwreck survivor on the sand.

My feet must have carried me of their own accord because suddenly I was back at the shop's front door, staring at the open sign. Maisie's heart-shaped face appeared in the window and she slowly opened the door to bring me inside.

"Cal, why don't you head home? Maybe get some sleep before the raid."

She said that so casually, like it was the next rainfall or the next workday. No, it was simply the next time bombs dropped out of the clouds. Our lives molded around daily trauma like moss overtaking a headstone.

A few customers browsing the shop paused to look at me.

"I'm fine," I said. "I'll just…work on some paperwork in the office."

I left the shop floor and flopped into the little chair in the office, letting my forehead rest on the desktop. My ledger was out under the counter, I realized, but I couldn't go back out there and get it. I didn't want Maisie to see me like that.

seven

Maisie

"We should go to the cinema on Sunday," Nora said from the end of my bed as she painted her fingernails. "I haven't been to the cinema in ages."

I glanced up from my magazine. "I'm not sure. I'm a little strapped for cash right now."

Nora blew on her fingertips and raised an eyebrow at me. "Are you sending money home to your parents?"

"Well, no—"

"Are you spending all your pocket money on comic books?" she asked in her soft estuary accent while grinning wide.

I laughed. "I spent all my money last weekend on a birthday gift for my mum."

Nora and I had become chummy recently but that didn't stop me from lying to her. Guilt crept up my arms as I flipped to the next page of my magazine and hid my face behind it.

"That's no problem, I'll pay for our tickets and you can get the tickets the next time." She beamed and blew on her nails again.

"Sure, sounds great."

Unfortunately, I didn't see myself having money for movie tickets in the near future. Not while I was cooking the shop's books, printing fake receipts, and slipping a portion of my earnings back into the cash register.

"Are you okay?" Nora screwed the cap back onto her coral nail polish bottle. "You seem a bit blue, love."

I tossed the magazine aside. "I'm worried about Cal. Something happened today and I think it really did a number on him."

"Oh?"

"Family stuff." I shrugged. "I don't think he'd like me telling people what happened."

"I don't know a single person that doesn't have one type of family trouble or another. I know I do."

Considering my family trouble, it seemed pretty mild in comparison to Cal's situation.

Nora was blowing on her fingertips again when Mrs. Martin appeared in the doorway, sniffing a few times. "What is that smell?"

Nora frowned at her and paused, giving Mrs. Martin a moment to figure out what she smelled on her own. It didn't work.

"Nail polish," Nora said flatly.

I snatched the magazine off the bed and hid my grin from behind its open pages.

"Smells wretched. That would give me a headache." She scoffed. "The siren will be going any minute. Best get to the shelter."

She left us to make our preparations and Nora rolled her eyes. "What a treasure she is."

I began my pre-raid routine: visit the toilet, brush my teeth, change into my nightdress and dressing gown, grab my pillow, put on my shoes, and head to the Anderson shelter. At first I was self-conscious about walking outside in my night clothes, but after only a couple weeks it felt very normal. I couldn't imagine being in my dressing gown in front of hundreds of people in an underground station shelter but I suppose a person got used to it there as well.

Nora and I made our nightly pilgrimage into the back garden, but I stopped when I noticed a light still on in the office. Slivers of its glow sneaked out from the edges of the blackout fabric over the stained glass window.

I sighed. "Cal must have left the light on when he left. Go on ahead, I'll be right there."

Nora nodded and joined Mrs. Martin in the shelter.

Before I could go back upstairs to fetch my keys, I heard movement from inside the shop. I knocked on the back door. Cal, his eyelids heavy and his shirt a little more rumpled and creased than usual, answered. He glanced at my dressing gown and quickly tore his eyes away.

"What on earth are you still doing here? The siren will be going off any—"

Naturally I was interrupted by the nightmare song of the siren.

"Blasted thing," he mumbled. "I must have fallen asleep at the desk. I only woke up when I heard you lot coming downstairs." He rubbed his eyes. "I need to get home."

"You'd better come to the Anderson with us tonight," I said, trying to speak over the pulsating siren.

"But there are only three bunks—"

"I can share with Nora. Stop being so stubborn," I snapped.

"And you should stop being so bossy."

I turned my head to glare at him but, to my surprise, found him smirking at me.

As we started for the shelter, a whistle echoed above. I grabbed Cal's arm to steady myself as the ground beneath our feet quaked, the bomb making impact. I didn't know where it landed but it couldn't have been far away—maybe two streets over, perhaps closer.

Cal followed me through the blackness of the garden, careful to avoid the raised vegetable patches. I pulled on the door handle of the shelter…and it didn't budge.

"Mrs. Martin, unlock the door," I heard Nora shout inside.

"Miss Beckett needs to learn a lesson in punctuality—"

"She could be killed out there! Open the door!"

Another whistle ripped through the sky and the earth shook again.

Cal grabbed my hand. "We don't have time for this. We can go to the shop cellar."

The shelter door remained closed, Nora's shouts at Mrs. Martin nearly drowned out by ambulance sirens.

Cal unlocked the back door, grabbed his torch from the office, and we hurried inside, down the stairs to the cellar. It smelled of must and damp, its dirt floors and concrete walls giving a less than homey feel to it—not that Mrs. Martin's Anderson shelter offered anything in the way of homey comforts either.

The cellar was split up into two rudimentary rooms; one was currently serving as the photo developing room and the other was used for storage—and, that night, shelter. Crates and boxes were stacked high along the walls. Grabbing two empty crates and flipping them over, Cal created two simple seats for us. I sat, hugging my pillow and blanket close.

Outside, the ack-ack of the anti-aircraft guns joined the cacophony above us and we both looked to the ceiling as it shuddered, spitting dust from between the beams.

"Why were you still at the office?"

"I told you, I fell asleep." He switched the torch off, plunging us into pitch black darkness. "Might as well save the batteries."

I hesitated. "Do you want to talk about what happened today with that woman?"

"No, I do not."

"Alright."

After a few minutes he turned on the torch again, handed it to me, and began organizing crates into two neat groups, each cluster three crates wide and five crates long.

"There. Beds," he said with a single nod. "Do watch for splinters."

He stretched out on one "bed" and rested his head on his bent arm.

"Here," I said, handing him my folded blanket. "I'll use my dressing gown."

"Oh. Thank you."

I clicked the torch off after I put my pillow in place. I slipped my dressing gown off and carefully positioned myself on the crates, trying to avoid sliding them out of place or getting stuck with a sharp edge or a nail. I wasn't entirely successful, as I managed to scratch my leg on something as I turned over on my side. I spread my dressing gown over myself and stared at the black void where I knew Cal was.

It could have been the complete darkness or the bombs and gunfire, but for some reason I briefly considered leaving my crates and sliding under the blanket with Cal. If a bomb dropped onto our building and it came crashing down upon us, at least I'd die in someone's arms. And they were quite nice arms, too; defined and solid.

Every time I began nodding off to sleep, a bomb blast from outside would bring me right back to the real world. It was still a bit early for sleep anyway but at that point, a person claimed sleep whenever and wherever they could get it.

"Her name is Susan."

"Hmm?"

"The young lady in the shop. My sister," Cal said. "Her name is Susan."

"Ah."

"She and I are almost the same age."

"Oh," I said and then, a moment later, "*oh*."

"Yes. Exactly." He sighed. "I had no idea my dad was unfaithful to my mum for so long before he left."

"Goodness." I didn't know what else to say.

"And my mum knows about Susan and never told me."

Cal gradually filled me in on his conversation with Susan, his voice quiet and solemn as he unspooled in the dark.

"How are you feeling about it all?"

"Confused mostly. Angry at my father all over again," he said. "It's difficult, having your father labeled as one specific type of person and then all of the sudden that label is changed entirely with no warning. Imagine one day, out of nowhere, you learned your father was—oh, I don't know—a communist. You'd end up examining various events in your life and how that event is now framed in your mind, knowing what you know now."

I very much wished to turn on the torch at that moment so I could see the look in his eyes and gauge how much he was hurting just then. Again, part of me wanted to relocate from my bed to his, curl in close and wrap my arms around him. Instead I remained, feeling helpless to ease his frustrations.

eight

CAL

Since I had a reliable coworker at the shop, I had a bit more freedom for the first time in ages. With so many Londoners volunteering with the war effort, I decided to lend a hand where I thought I would be useful.

More and more homes and businesses were hit by bombs every night, obliterating many in a flash, leaving only shattered glass, splintered wood, and dust. However, some buildings managed to only sustain minor damage. Finding supplies to fix salvageable houses and shopfronts was a huge challenge, nearly impossible, but patching them up with found and makeshift materials or helping with clearing debris was slightly easier. That's where me and a few other lads came in.

"Oy, Woodbury," one of the other crew members yelled from across the room, his cockney accent thick, "'elp me with this, would ya?"

I grabbed one end of the huge tarpaulin he was hauling, and we dragged it up two flights of stairs to a bedroom that had a rather large hole in the ceiling. The room already survived one night of rain, but at least with some kind of slapdash ceiling there was a chance it might dry out a bit and not be ruined entirely. We could only try.

The next building we were sent to was only a few streets from the shop; a three-storey home that looked as if it had been ripped down the middle by an angry giant. It was the type of assignment I hated the most—we were to look for human remains before clearing as much debris from the street and pavement as possible. By the time we got to a lot of bomb sites, the chances of finding someone still alive was extremely low.

"I found one lady buried under her house, but she died as we were pulling her out," one of the crew told me on my first day. "Finding an arm or a torso is hard but at least you don't have to watch 'em die first."

It had been a day and a half since I'd woken up in a dark cellar, my back sore from sleeping on wooden crates all night. I'd considered waking Maisie up but her shallow little breaths sounded so peaceful; I figured it might be wiser to let her sleep. I'd left my torch beside her in case she woke up and didn't know where she was. I made a mental note to find some candles and matches and store them there just in case.

Wiping my forehead with the back of my arm, I winced as a trickle of perspiration ran down my spine. I slung my sweat-soaked shirts over the arm of the wheelbarrow, slicked my damp hair back with my palm and went back to loading shovelfuls of rubble—what I guessed had once upon a time been bricks—into a wheelbarrow.

I heard a giggle behind me. "You look a little warm."

Looking over my shoulder, I grinned. "Perhaps a little."

Maisie, strolling toward me in a yellow floral print dress, looked like a summer day. A little yellow bow kept her thick brown curls at bay and a shopping bag bounced against her thigh as she walked.

The Maisie who visited me in my dreams would no longer wear a black dress. From then on, it was that yellow dress.

Her eyes lingered on my bare torso before tracing a path up my arm, her cheeks flushing when her eyes met mine. I rubbed the back of my neck and let out a short chuckle, suddenly feeling self-conscious about my shirtless state. Maisie didn't seem to mind it though.

In fact, if I wasn't mistaken, she was having a hard time *not* looking at my chest and abdomen.

"Shopping today?" I nodded at her bag.

"A few essentials. I managed to find some batteries for your torch.

Thank you for leaving it for me the other night." She laughed. "I would have likely walked into a wall without it." She looked at the remaining walls of the home beside us, its bricks now a jumble of dusty rocks on the pavement, impeding foot traffic. Her eyes were wide, taking in all the details of its destruction, genuine sorrow in her eyes. "I loved this house. What a terrible, tragic waste." She looked back at me. "And you get to see all of it firsthand."

"I figured I should help where I could."

I silently hoped she wouldn't ask me why I wasn't in uniform again, and she didn't. I knew she was probably still wondering but thankfully gave up asking.

"Maisie, I wanted to thank you for…letting me get some things off my chest the other night." I cleared my throat. "I had no right to open up about my family troubles to you. I wanted you to know I appreciated it. Truly."

"Of course. I hope it helped you to feel better." She gave a little shrug, a shy smile on her crimson lips.

God, I would have given anything to kiss those lips.

"It helped, I think—"

The tiniest scrap of a sound caught my attention and I stopped speaking, focusing my efforts on identifying where it came from. Maisie tilted her head, her eyes scanning the debris littering the surrounding area.

"Is that a cat?" I put my shovel aside and stepped closer to the pile a few feet away.

"It's probably scared to death or hurt," she exclaimed, dropping her shopping bag on the pavement, her eyes studying the mound of wreckage.

Please don't let the cat be maimed too badly. I don't want Maisie to see that.

The cat let out a pathetic little squeak and Maisie and I immediately began picking up bits of rock and chunks of splintered wood. Maisie coughed into her sleeve as the dust rose, but she kept on digging. The cat meowed, sensing us getting closer.

Suddenly a tiny orange and white face appeared, and it meowed as loudly as its little body would allow but it was still trapped inside by something. Its tiny dirty paws stretched out to us, crying for help, its whiskers and fur coated in filth.

"Don't pull so, my darling," Maisie cooed to the creature in a soft voice. "We'll get you out, I promise."

I pushed away the remaining debris. "He must have crawled inside a basket during the raid." I carefully lifted the shredded chunk of wicker the cat was clinging to, its little leg turned at an unnatural angle. "Oh, dear. I think he has a broken leg." I held him close and petted his head as he squirmed against me.

"Oh, no, you poor thing," Maisie exclaimed, leaning close to me to examine the kitten. "I'll take it to a veterinarian right now. Do you know where the nearest clinic would be?" She grabbed her bag and held it open.

By this point, the yowling kitten clung to my bare shoulder with his claws and I winced while supporting him with one hand. I grabbed one of my shirts from the wheelbarrow and threw it in the bag first to give the cat something soft to lay on.

"There's one four streets down that way." I nodded my head to the right. "I think it's next to a pet store."

Maisie cradled the kitten on my shoulder and carefully pulled him off of me, setting him in the bag with my shirt. She cradled the bag in both arms and frowned.

"You might want to put something on that," she said, pointing at the tiny bleeding puncture marks on my shoulder. "Talk to you tomorrow!" She sprinted down the pavement, holding her bag tight to her chest.

"Who was *that*?"

I whipped around to see Francis, one of the crew lads, grinning wide at me and leaning on a shovel. He and I were the youngest on our crew and became chums quickly.

"She works at the shop with me," I said firmly, picking up my shovel again. "And don't even think about it."

"Think about what? I was only asking who she was." He shrugged. "Some nice gams on that girl though."

"I suppose so, yes."

"If she's just your coworker, maybe you should introduce us."

I gave him a stern look of warning over my shoulder.

"Oh, I see." He laughed loudly behind me. "I don't think I'd stand a chance anyway. I saw the way she looked at you."

I didn't look back at him to give him the satisfaction. Instead, I smiled as I worked.

nine

Maisie

"How's your furry little friend?" Nora picked at her Woolton pie.

"Better. He was a little sore for the first few days but he's getting around quite well now," I said. "He's a survivor, that one."

"What furry friend is that?" Mrs. Martin glared at me. "I told you I don't allow pets in this house."

I slowly turned to her, feeling a tenseness in my jaw. "I know. That's why he's living with Cal at his flat."

Cal and I came to an agreement that since I couldn't keep the kitten, I would pay for his veterinary bills and Cal would keep him at his flat and feed him. Of course, he agreed to that while not knowing a large chunk of my income went directly back in the store's till when he wasn't looking. He didn't know how tight my purse strings had to be for a while after that costly visit to the animal clinic. Too tight, really.

"Good," she snapped. "I don't like cats. Their fur gets everywhere, and they kill birds. I don't like dogs either. The barking gives me a headache."

Nora's lips puckered. I could tell she was trying to withhold a smirk. "How do you feel about pet birds?"

"Oh, I don't like them one bit. They carry diseases. They shouldn't be pets at all, that's what I say." Mrs. Martin gave a resolute nod.

"Quite right." Nora glanced back at me and I choked down my urge to laugh. "That was very kind of Cal to take the kitten in. What a sweet gesture," she said, stuffing her grinning mouth with the last of her vegetables.

"Yes," I said firmly, giving her a warning look. "It was very kind of him."

Nora had begun the very irritating habit of giving me a very specific expression every time Cal's name was brought up in conversation. I hadn't even told her about seeing Cal without a shirt on the day when we found the kitten.

And I certainly didn't tell her about how many times I'd thought about what he looked like without a shirt on.

And I absolutely didn't mention all the ways my body responded when I saw him that day, his bare torso glistening in the sun.

"It's almost like he fancies you or something," she whispered.

"It's not like that at all." I shook my head. "I think the cat claimed him as his own and Cal just went along with it."

"Sure. That's probably it," she added in a playful tone. "Did the two of you name the kitten?"

"Cal is calling him—"

"Aphrodite?" Nora suggested. "Valentine? Cupid? Oh, perhaps Venus? Or—"

"Tiger," I interrupted.

She shrugged. "That's not very romantic."

"Naming stray cats," Mrs. Martin chimed in, clearing our dishes from the table. "What foolishness."

Mrs. Martin turned on the wireless as she did dishes, and Nora and I knew better than to try to talk when the wireless was on.

"The Germans could be invading this second and I wouldn't even know about it because you two couldn't stop gossiping while I'm trying to hear the news," she barked at the two of us shortly after I moved in.

"You really think the BBC would announce the Nazis were on their way during *The Kitchen Front?*" Nora quipped. "Here's how to make a plum pudding and oh, by the way, Hitler just landed at Dover?"

That comment earned Nora a wicked glare from Mrs. Martin and a punishment of no sugar for her tea the following day. In retaliation, Nora stole "emergency sugar" from the larder the following night in case Mrs. Martin pulled that trick again.

Up in Nora's bedroom, she hand mended a small hole in the seam of a skirt while I sat on her bed.

"I never thought I'd be so grateful I can sew," she said, pulling a long stitch through the precious garment. "Clothes will be the next thing to be on the ration. I'd bet good money on that." She suddenly looked up from her mending, her eyes bright. "We never went to that movie, you know. Maybe we could go this weekend?"

"That kitten's veterinary visit used up every cent I had. Which reminds me…" I winced. "Any chance I could borrow five bob? I hate to even ask. I get paid on Friday—"

"It's alright. Of course I can lend you money." She frowned. "Is Cal not paying you enough?"

I hesitated and bit the corner of my lip. "It's complicated."

She arched a perfectly shaped eyebrow. "It's not *that* complicated."

Sighing, I rested my head on the wall behind me and explained the shop's financial difficulties and my need to keep the shop going no matter what. And then I admitted to secretly putting a portion of my wages back.

Nora looked at me like I was a child who had spelled their own name incorrectly. "I hate to be the one to tell you this, darling, but if the shop isn't making enough money for the two employees it needs to run, then it's not really working out as well as you'd hoped."

"I know, I know. The plan was daft. Believe me, I know," I huffed. "I thought once we had a photo developing room set up downstairs, it would bring in more income based on services rather than expensive products, so it would make more profit but it's taking a while to get the word out. Maybe I should tell Cal to put an ad in the paper."

"Or maybe Londoners don't want to capture their memories on film from *this* particular time in their lives." She tied the thread off and snipped. "The bombs and all. Deaths of friends and loved ones and so on." She looked up and saw my devastated expression. "Sorry, love."

"No, you're right," I said. "I should have considered that before I set the room up."

Nora put her scissors and thread away. "How do you know how to develop photos anyway? Is that a common service to offer in village shops?"

"My aunt taught me. She's the reason the shop had all the development stuff in the first place. She was a photographer."

"Is she no longer a photographer?"

"She died when I was fifteen," I said. "She taught me development *and* photography, actually."

"Darling, I'm sorry. If you don't mind me asking, how did she die?"

I hated explaining the event when people asked. Lying and saying something like "cancer" or "she was struck by lightning" seemed much simpler.

"Jean did all kinds of photography, but she won several prizes for her risky nature photography. One day she went to take photos of some seaside cliffs and she slipped on a rock and fell."

"Oh, my goodness. That's terrible!"

"The worst day of my life." It had been seven years and describing how she died still made my throat sting and constrict.

"I'm so sorry, Maisie," Nora breathed. "I shouldn't have brought it up."

"No, it's alright. She was a wonderful person and not telling people about her seems unfair to her memory."

After a few minutes of uncomfortable silence, Nora looked up. "You never told me you were a photographer."

"Oh, I'm not," I said. "I've barely touched a camera since then."

Nora joined me on the bed. "Did your aunt teach you how to do portraits?"

"She did but like I said, it's been years—"

"Do you think you could remember how to do it?" She leaned forward.

"Well, I-I suppose I probably—Wait, why are you asking?"

Nora was practically glowing by that point. "I have a couple of friends who are looking to hire a portrait photographer."

"That shouldn't be too difficult here."

"You see, the type of portrait photography they're looking for is a bit—" She searched for the right word. "—indecent?"

I felt my eyes grow wide. "Pardon?"

She shook her head and flicked a dismissive hand. "Nothing *too* bawdy. They're both looking for portraits that are a bit…um… seductive. You know, to send to their men serving in the war."

She grabbed a magazine from her bedside table and flipped to a photo of the Hollywood actress Hedy Lamarr, posing in a chic gown and making love to the camera with her entrancing eyes.

"I see."

"You could do it," she said, her speech speeding up. "It would be easy money. You can take the pictures and I'll do hair, makeup, and provide clothing if they can't bring their own. Not that finding makeup is easy right now, but I think I can fake the look of mascara and lipstick at the very least. We could do the photo shoot on Sunday when we're both off work. We'd have to find a place to shoot the photos. Maybe if it goes well, we could make it an ongoing side gig—"

"Nora." I winced. "I can't. I'm sorry."

She blinked at me a few times. "Not even the one time with my friends? They're nice girls. They wouldn't tell a soul if that's what you're worried about."

"It's not that. Well, it's not that entirely," I corrected. "I don't do photography anymore. When I was younger I thought I wanted to be a photographer like Jean, but after she died I lost interest in it. I don't think I could just pick it up again. And if I were to try it again, I don't think I could start with a paying photography job right out of the gate. That's far too much pressure." I lowered my chin. "I really am very sorry to disappoint you."

She shrugged. "No, *I'm* sorry. I shouldn't have thrown the idea at you like that." She straightened her shoulders. "We'll come up with something else you can do to make a little extra money on the side."

"I should be out volunteering, not trying to take on a second paying job." Nora and I had previously enquired at the Women's Voluntary Service about helping out at our local rest shelter, but they told us there was already a waitlist for the WVS.

"You're giving back part of your wages so the shop doesn't collapse. You're *already* volunteering."

I laughed. "'Collapse' might be a bit of an exaggeration."

Soon after I went to my room for a nap before the eventual air raid siren went. That was the nineteenth night in a row the German planes came to London bringing bombs, fire, and chaos. Death and destruction.

As I listened to Mrs. Martin's snores, Nora's wakeful tossing and turning in the bunk above mine, and the aural bedlam of the terrors outside, I considered her offer.

I was sure taking a few silly, risqué photos of Nora's friends would be fine, as long as nobody found out. However, if the photos came out nicely, I knew I might want to do it again and maybe again after that. I'd already put that dream behind me a long time ago in order to focus on something more reliable, something safer.

I certainly missed photography. But I missed Aunt Jean more.

ten

CAL

"How long has it been since you saw Roy?"

Maisie thought for a moment, the broom in her hands going still. "I'm not sure. Maybe four or five months?" The soft scraping of the broom began again. "He's shipping out again next week, so he wanted to see us before then. He was lucky to get leave for the whole weekend."

I nodded and continued doing some last-minute book work. "Why don't you call it a day? You probably need to catch your train."

She brought the broom back to the front counter. "Are you sure?"

"No, I'm just saying that to be nice," I said, glancing up from my ledger. "Look at all the customers in here needing help this instant." I gestured to the empty shop floor.

Her eyes lit up as she smiled, and my stomach fluttered.

Do it now. Do it now, you coward.

"Maybe on Monday night when you get back to London, you and I could—"

The bell above the entrance jingled frantically as a customer whipped the door open. The blue Royal Navy uniform was the first thing I noticed. Maisie glanced over her shoulder and then, her eyes growing large, she gasped and threw her arms around the sailor's neck. He dropped his suitcase and squeezed her, giving her a kiss on the top of her head.

"I thought you were going straight to Mum and Dad's," Maisie exclaimed. "What are you doing here?"

Roy Beckett flashed his movie star smile, his cheeks a suspicious rosy hue. "I wanted to surprise you." He gave me a friendly nod. "And I wanted to check on the shop, of course. Glad to see you two keeping the ol' place up and running while I'm gone."

Maisie rolled her eyes. "You were drinking with your Navy friends, weren't you?"

"Quite possibly."

I joined the two of them by the door and Roy clapped me on the back. "It's good to see you."

"And you! How was your first trip out to sea?"

The tiniest flicker of reluctance passed across his eyes. That and his slight pause told me everything I needed to know.

"I managed not to get seasick, which is more than I can say for some of the other lads," he said with a forced laugh.

"The uniform suits you," Maisie said, giving him the once over. "You look taller somehow."

"Tell that to the girls we were trying to impress at the pub," he scoffed. "They only had eyes for those boys in the RAF. Bloody blighters making us all look bad."

I snickered. He wasn't wrong. The pilots flying Spitfires and Hurricanes in the Royal Air Force, battling the Luftwaffe in the sky, were idolized by all for their bravery. I'd heard multiple stories about RAF pilots taking full advantage of their popularity with women as well, dating and shagging as many as possible.

"I'll go get my suitcase and then we can head to the train station," Maisie said, sending me a sweet smile on her way out the door. "Thanks again, Cal."

I nodded and watched her whisk down the pavement to the door leading up to the flat. When I looked back at Roy, he had one eyebrow arched.

"You two getting along?"

"Not at first but we're making it work now."

He crossed his arms over his wide chest, his eyes narrowing slightly.

"What?"

"You don't fancy her, do you?"

An uncomfortable laugh escaped my lips. "Maisie? Of course not."

"Because you looked at her like she…well, like she's not my sister."

I waited for him to laugh or smile or something. Anything. But he kept glowering at me.

"No," I said finally. "Nothing has happened between Maisie and I."

His face stayed still as stone.

"She just works here," I quickly added, desperate to fill the silence between us.

"Glad to hear it." He gave a single nod. "And nothing *will* happen, right?"

I opened my mouth to speak as Maisie opened the front door, suitcase in hand, huffing a little from rushing up and down the stairs.

"Ready?" She beamed up at her brother before looking back at me. "I just realized I won't have to listen to bombs for two nights in a row! It'll be so nice to sleep in a real bed."

I nodded, not sure how I was allowed to respond with Roy watching me.

Roy's face, significantly softer by then, picked up his suitcase again. "Let's go."

"Have a nice weekend, Cal," Maisie called as Roy shut the door and the two of them passed by the windows.

Roy flashed me one last warning glare before disappearing from view.

"That stupid uniform makes you look like a prat," I muttered under my breath.

I let out a long exhale and stared at the ceiling, all the profanity I knew running through my mind. Roy had no right to decide if Maisie and I shouldn't date.

I mindlessly hung up the blackout curtains, finished sweeping, locked the doors, and headed home, my mind slingshotting from one line of reasoning to another.

Roy and I were like brothers as children. When I moved to London, he visited me as much as possible, even though he didn't have to. He had lots of friends in Hazeldon that could have easily taken my place. But he wanted to be there for me when I was at my most miserable.

Besides all that, I owed Roy my life.

Not asking Maisie out to dinner wasn't that much to ask of a friend, I thought as I unlocked the door to my flat.

I tried to consider how I'd feel if Roy suddenly fancied *my* sister. As an only child, I couldn't really make any true comparison.

But I *wasn't* an only child—not anymore. But I was far from seeing Susan the way Roy saw Maisie. Susan wasn't my *real* sister and she never would be.

It wasn't like Maisie was the only lovely girl in London. There were more single girls looking for a good time in the city than ever before and hardly any other young men around to compete with. Honestly, I was foolish by developing an attraction to Maisie in the first place.

Hours went by and I remained deep in thought. Sirens shrieked out into the English sky and I made my nightly pilgrimage to the building's cellar, a pillow under one arm and a blanket under the other. As I propped my pillow against the wall in my usual spot and listened to the war raging above our heads, I had a bleak realization.

Maybe Roy thinks I'm unworthy of his sister. And maybe he's absolutely right.

eleven

Maisie

Since Hazeldon was located just outside of Guildford in Surrey, a train from London was usually a reasonably short affair. Transportation going almost anywhere had been delayed and interrupted thanks to the nightly bombing raids. Luckily, our train ride was smooth and on time.

"What was it like being out at sea for so long?"

There it was again—the same hesitant look in Roy's eyes he had when I asked him about making new friends during training.

"Quiet at times. Stressful at other times," he said.

"Did you see any U-boats?"

"If we could see the damn things in the first place, that would make our lives much easier."

He glanced at the pretty blonde lady sitting across from us pretending to read an Agatha Christie novel, all the while eyeing Roy since the moment we boarded the train. The two locked eyes for a moment before she lowered her gaze again to her book.

I shook my head at him. "Subtle."

He gave a little shrug. "What about you? I hope Cal isn't making you work too hard. He can be a bit of a stickler sometimes."

"It's been good. I like working there," I said. "It's quite different selling luxury goods compared to selling essentials." I noticed his attention had wandered back to the blonde woman. "Alligators come into the shop on occasion."

"Mmm. Right." Roy nodded, his eyes still on the woman's calves as she crossed her legs.

I sighed loudly. "You've been at sea for two months, Roy, not two years."

Roy turned to me sharply, annoyed. The blonde woman tightened her red lips, smothering a grin.

"She's my sister, by the way," he said to the woman, giving a friendly nod. "And I'm Roy."

She stuck out her dainty gloved hand. "Anna. Nice to meet you."

Roy shook her hand and the two of them chatted while I leaned my head against the window and watched the outside world fly by. Roy only turned back to me when Anna departed the train at Guildford, but not before giving Roy her phone number and address on a little slip of paper. He'd always been good at wooing but watching my brother flirt was enough to make my stomach turn.

He smiled smugly at me, tucking the little slip of paper into his pocket.

"That was repulsive to watch."

"It was a *long* two months, Maisie." He shrugged. "You wouldn't understand."

"I'm sure I don't."

The train soon arrived at Hazeldon and Roy carried our suitcases, his shoulders pushed further back than usual, his head higher. He must have known every person on the high street was watching us and seeing his crisp blue Navy uniform. As we walked by the village shop, I fought the urge to run in and check on things, just to make sure everything was running smoothly in my absence. I decided I better not or else I might end up stocking shelves or chatting with a customer about my "big move up to London" for an hour.

"So, Cal is being nice to you and all that?"

"Of course."

"Because you should know Cal is nice to everyone," he said quickly.

"Some girls get the wrong idea sometimes."

"What's that supposed to mean?"

"It's not that Cal *means* to lead girls on. He'd never do it intentionally of course. But some girls assume when a lad is nice to them, well, they sometimes think it means something more than what it actually means."

I stopped walking. "Did Cal *say* something to you?"

"No—"

"Then why are you hinting at something? Why are you being odd?"

"I don't want you to get your hopes up when it comes to Cal."

"I don't have any hopes of any kind in regards to Calvin Woodbury, alright?"

That wasn't strictly true, but my brother didn't need to know that.

"Good," he said as we started walking again.

"Good." I forced a tone of casualness into my voice. "Speaking of Cal, why isn't he serving in the war?"

Roy glanced down at me, pausing before he answered. "He has syphilis."

"He does *not*."

"He does," he quipped. "He'll probably deny it entirely if you ever ask him about it though, which you shouldn't because it's a very sensitive subject."

At the sight of her baby boy in the doorway, Mum burst into tears. With her arms wrapped around Roy, she repeatedly kissed his cheek and held his face in her hands to get a good look at him.

"I'm so happy you're here," she said with a sob. She wiped the tears from her cheeks with the back of her hand and looked behind Roy to see me. "Hi dear. Could you set the table for me? Your father will be home soon."

Picking up my suitcase from where Roy set it by the front door, I lugged it upstairs to my old bedroom. I was surprised to find Mum's sewing machine set up on my desk and a neatly folded stack of fabric on my chair. The few photos previously hanging on the walls were gone, replaced with a few watercolor paintings of flowers.

With narrowed eyes, I backed out of the room and glanced quickly around my brother's old bedroom next door. Not a thing was out of place since he moved out a few years before. His athletic medals and trophies were still displayed prominently on a shelf by the window. Even the stack of comic books on his bedside table had a noticeable coating of dust along the edges.

I had only been gone a month and already my bedroom was being co-opted by my mother.

Back downstairs, I set the table for the four of us while Mum busied herself in the kitchen, finishing up dinner.

"I traded my secret pie recipes to get this ham and enough eggs for the cake we're having for dessert," I overheard Mum telling Roy. "So you better enjoy it."

Of course Mum made his favorite. Only the best for her boy.

Dad arrived home shortly after. I was in the dining room, setting out "the good plates" as instructed, while they had their reunion.

"This war will be over by Christmas," I heard Dad say. "The Hun couldn't beat us before, they certainly won't beat us now."

Like many men his age, my father served in the Great War. In fact, he was still in France when I was born. At fifty, he was too old for war duty and as the owner of several shops, he was too busy to join the Home Guard.

The two of them found me in the dining room as Dad headed for his stash of spirits.

He smiled wide at me before his head disappeared into his liquor cabinet. "It's so nice to have the two of you here together like old times."

The glass bottles in his cabinet clinked together as he looked for something special. Once he found it, he stood upright and inspected the bottle, holding it further away from himself in order to read the label.

"Dad, your glasses," I said gently.

He rolled his eyes and took his spectacles from around his neck, setting them no higher than the very tip of his nose. "Yes, that's the one. Sweetheart, can you bring us two glasses before you help your mum with dinner?"

"Of course."

I ignored the twinge of jealousy I felt as I fetched the glasses from the kitchen. That jealousy was nothing new and it was a feeling I learned to cope with many years before.

A few minutes later, Mum and I added steaming bowls of potatoes and carrots to the table. Everything smelled incredible. Going by the amount of food between us, I realized Dad must have used his connections with the local farmers to get a little extra for that dinner—it was far beyond what a ration book could likely provide.

"Tell me everything," Dad said to Roy. The tip of Dad's nose was rosy from whatever spirits they'd imbibed together. "It must be so exciting."

Roy shrugged. "Sometimes."

"We heard about what happened to the *City of Benares*," Mum said between bites. "Scared me half to death. I don't know how many calls I made to make sure you weren't on that ship." She shook her head.

The joy drained from Roy's eyes. "Two of my friends were."

"I'm sorry to hear that," Dad said. "Just know that they died in the most honorable way a man can die—by serving his country."

Once the bombing raids began in London, a lot of families were anxious to get their children to safety in Canada. The week before our family dinner, the SS *City of Benares*, carrying ninety children in addition to their chaperones and the crew, was struck by a German torpedo, sinking within minutes. Some survivors were found in a lifeboat eight days later but most of the children had tragically been lost to a watery grave.

"I can't imagine sending a child away so they can be safe, only to learn they drowned in the Atlantic," Mum added, shaking her head.

Roy and I exchanged looks over the table. He lowered his eyes and slowly chewed.

"Like I said," Dad interjected, his tone upbeat, "the war will be over before you know it, and you'll be back in London at the shop in no time."

My shoulders tensed. I kept my eyes on my plate.

"Cal told me Maisie is doing a good job at the shop," Roy said.

I smiled weakly.

Dad gave a firm nod. "Of course she is. But once the war is over, life can get back to normal, like how it was before."

But what if I don't want life to be like it was before?

"Right," Roy said quietly. Clearing his throat, he added, "I hope you don't mind, I'm meeting Walt and Bill at the pub in an hour."

Walt and Bill were longtime friends of his. Both of them were farmers so were exempted from war conscription.

It was Mum and Dad's turn to exchange looks over the table.

"Of course it's fine, dear," Mum said, her eyes fixed on her water glass. "You have fun with your friends."

Dad sighed out of his nose—the telltale sign of his displeasure.

"How is Doris doing with managing the shop?" I was desperate to break the tension.

"Good enough I suppose. I think the customers miss you though," Dad said. "It'll be good when you can come back."

A heat rose in my chest as I stared at my father's forehead. He was too busy separating the potatoes from the carrots on his plate with his fork to notice.

I left Hazeldon because he wanted me to. Now he obviously wanted me back at the village shop and Roy back in London. I was giving up my wages to make sure his beloved hobby shop survived. Not that he knew about that.

And his continuous claims the war would be over in no time? Had he not read a newspaper in the last year? Perhaps he would have felt different if he'd spent every night of the last month listening to bombs and air raid sirens instead of being safely tucked up in the country.

The Monday train trip back to London felt like a blur. As I walked from the train station, I noticed several more buildings were destroyed in the two nights I had spent away.

I had expected to sleep well in my old bed, in my old bedroom, in my old house, in my old village. I'd lain awake staring at the ceiling, my jaw aching from clenching for hours.

Instead of going to Barnaby Street right away, I stopped at the seamstress shop a few streets over to see Nora. Since she was the only employee around, I let myself behind the front counter and leaned against a nearby storage cabinet of sewing notions.

She arched an eyebrow at me. "I was about to ask how the Hazeldon visit was but I think I already know the answer to that question."

"Is it that obvious?"

She gave an innocent little shrug.

I raised my suitcase slightly. "I brought my camera with me from home. We'll need it if we're going to do some portraits."

twelve

CAL

October arrived in London and, with it, the German planes continued their nightly assaults on the city. I kept myself busy on my days off by cleaning up the debris of family homes and businesses, trying to keep my conflicted thoughts and feelings buried.

Maisie did not make that easy.

She leaned over the front of the counter and beamed up at me with those big brown eyes of hers, partially obscured by long black eyelashes. "What did you get up to last night?"

"Well, if you must know, some Nazis showed up and I ended up spending a lovely evening in the basement with my neighbors—"

"I meant before the raid. I'm tired of people talking about bombs and fires and destroyed houses. It's constant." She disappeared into the back room and dragged the blackout curtain out to be hung up.

"Well, pardon us for being a little preoccupied with the destruction happening around us."

She looked at me over her shoulder. "What did you do after work and before the raid? What do you do for fun?"

Lowering my eyes to my ledger, I scratched in a random number in a random column to give the impression of being busy. "I went for a run."

Maisie retrieved a stool from the back room. "You run?"

"Yes. I like to run."

Running was my preferred exercise since I was about twelve. A lonely kid didn't need to make plans to meet up with friends he didn't have—besides Roy who couldn't always be around—in order to go for a run. It got my blood pumping without the need for competitiveness or aggression. I did some of my best thinking while running.

"Where did you run to?"

"I wasn't running *to* anywhere in particular, but I ran in Hyde Park," I said. "Or, rather, what's left of it."

Many of London's parks had been co-opted by the war effort. Part of Hyde Park's lovely greenery was turned into a large vegetable patch while other parks hosted anti-aircraft guns, military lodgings, or public shelters. It was like nothing in the entire city was beyond the long arm of the war.

I subtly watched Maisie from the corner of my eye as she hung the blackout curtain, capturing the perfection of her calves and the sublime roundness of her ass. Quickly looking away, I silently cursed myself.

Don't even look at her. It's not worth it.

While I made dinner that night, tiny drizzle droplets dotted the window over the kitchen sink. I weighed my options while Tiger pressed his body into the backs of my legs.

I could put my lifelong friendship with Roy first, continue leering at Maisie wantonly and having rather inappropriate dreams about her every night until I eventually get over my silly infatuation.

I could put my friendship with Roy at risk and ask Maisie to dinner. She could easily decline, making our working relationship extremely uncomfortable, if not impossible to maintain.

Or…

Or I could tell Roy to go to Hell and then one day grab Maisie around the waist and kiss her until she feels faint. This would, of course, be followed by Maisie turning the Open sign over in the window and leaping into my open arms. With her creamy thighs around my waist, I would carry her to the office, set her on top of the desk and show her exactly how I felt about her.

My groin ached at the thought and I considered going to deal with it properly.

But then there was a knock at the door.

I cursed, adjusted myself, opened the door and then immediately wished I had not answered the knock.

Damp from the rain and wearing civilian clothes, Roy Beckett stood in the hallway. He carried a duffle bag and obviously hadn't shaved in a day or two.

I stared at him, baffled and wondering if this was some kind of nightmare, a prank, or some twisted combination of the two.

"Aren't you going to invite me in?" He slid past me into my flat, tossing his bag down by the coat rack.

I slowly closed the door and turned to face him. "Did you get extra time for leave?"

"What are you cooking? Smells good." Roy peered into the bubbling pan on the stove. "Smells better than it looks."

"Why are you not in uniform?"

He took a seat on the couch, stretching his arm over the back of it. He gave a little bounce to gauge its condition. "Not bad."

"Why are you here?" I asked, louder this time.

"Blimey, Maisie was right," he said, frowning at me. "You are a bit of a prig now, aren't you?"

"She didn't say that, did she?" I shook my head. "Never mind. What are you doing?" I switched off the hob and turned back around to face him.

He released a long breath, his shoulders slumping. "You don't know what it's like."

"You're right. I don't. I wish I did."

"No, you don't," Roy said, looking directly at me, his words crisp and sharp. "You might think you would be better off on some ship in the middle of the Atlantic or out there in the mud or in a plane or in some godforsaken dessert, serving like other men, but you don't bloody know what it's like." He clenched as he spoke. "You don't know how lucky you are."

He wasn't the one being asked every single day by customers why he wasn't serving in the war and why he wasn't wearing a uniform. *He* wasn't looked at like he was a traitor to his country or a coward.

"What happened?"

He lowered his gaze to the floor. "Two of my friends from basic were on the *City of Benares* when it sank. They were seventeen." He looked back up at me. "Seventeen. Dead, just like that. It could have been me."

"That's horrible. I'm so sorry."

"There was one U-boat tailing us for days, but it disappeared suddenly. I keep thinking, 'But what if it hadn't?'" He rifled in his pants pocket for his cigarettes and lit one, his hand quivering slightly. He shook his head and blew smoke from the corner of his mouth. "I'm not goin' out like that."

I sat on the couch next to him. "Do they know you…" I struggled to avoid the word 'deserted.' "Do they know you're missing?"

"I was supposed to board a ship this morning but instead I came to London. I couldn't do it. I just couldn't do it." He took another long drag and closed his eyes. "Seventeen," he repeated.

"They died as heroes." I regretted saying it as soon as the words escaped. It's just what you were supposed to say in those sad situations.

He shot me a glare, one I knew I deserved. "There is nothing heroic or honorable about being hunted down like a fox by something you can't even bloody see. That ship was full of kids and those bastards sank it anyway. There's no glory in sea water filling your lungs as you scream into the dark, surrounded by dying children."

The tremor of Roy's hand became more intense as he lifted his cigarette to his lips again. "I can't go back." He finally looked at me. "You have to help me."

"They're going to come here to look for you. Where am I supposed to hide you? What if they find you?"

"I'd rather be alive in prison than dead on a Navy ship."

"Will I go to prison too if they find you here?"

"Probably." Roy shook his head. "I'm sorry to put you in this position but I have nowhere else to go."

There were a million panicked thoughts racing through my head. "I spend nights in the basement with my neighbors during air raids, but you can't come with me."

"I'll go to a shelter instead. I won't talk to anyone."

"What about food rations?"

"We'll manage. I'll pick up odd jobs—"

"But you can't leave the flat."

"I can't stay in here all day—"

"You have to," I snarled before lowering my voice. "We should speak quietly as well, and you have to stay silent during the day. The neighbors will be suspicious if there is suddenly someone else in my flat during the day."

A flicker of hesitation crossed over Roy's face. He nodded. "Alright."

Neither of us said anything for a moment as we both considered what a terrible situation we just entered into.

"Hopefully the war doesn't last too long." I smiled weakly.

He rose from the couch and took a final drag from his cigarette, stubbing it out in the sink. He stood a moment looking out of the kitchen window.

"You can't tell Maisie I'm here," he finally said.

I joined him in the kitchen to avoid yelling across my flat, even though the urge to scream at him was becoming rapidly stronger.

"She's going to find out you're missing soon enough, and she's going to figure out where you are. She's not an idiot," I said.

"If she asks you if I'm here, you have to lie to her," he said. "You have to lie to her to keep her in the dark, to protect her."

"But—"

"If she knows where I am, she won't give me up. I know she wouldn't. But I can't risk being found and having the authorities find out she was involved. I won't do that."

"You'll risk me but not her?" I cocked an eyebrow.

"Yes, exactly," he said, a little too casually. "It's either this or you injure me badly enough they won't take me back."

"I could give it a go." I shrugged in mock indifference. "Which eye do you prefer, your left or your right?"

I barely slept that night. At first I could easily blame it on the bombs. After the raid ended and the all clear sounded in the wee hours, I trudged back to my flat and waited for Roy to come back from the shelter.

After a few minutes, I began frantically checking the hall for him. My head ached from exhaustion and my body yearned for sleep. I eventually gave up and collapsed onto my unmade bed. Even when I heard Roy return a few minutes later, locking the door behind him, sleep would not come. Roy's soft snoring from the couch reached me and still, sleep would not come. Early morning light crept into my room from the edges of my blackout curtains and still, sleep would not come.

This is a very, very bad idea.

thirteen

Maisie

I was eating a bland breakfast of tea and dry toast with Nora and Mrs. Martin when the bell in the living room chimed.

The bell at Mrs. Martin's flat was actually a clever little rig her son set up for her years before. The knocker on the street level front door was tied with a string. This string ran along the ceiling of the staircase that led from that door to a little bell—similar to the kind hanging above the door in the hobby shop—in Mrs. Martin's living room.

Mrs. Martin glared in the direction of the sound. "At this time of day?" She slid her chair back from the table with a screech and went to the window, peering down to the street. "It's two men in black uniforms."

My stomach dropped, and my toast fell from my hand. Nora and I exchanged worried looks.

Mrs. Martin looked over her shoulder. "You better go talk to them, Miss Beckett."

The walk down the stairs to the front door was a blur, yet it felt like a mile-long trudge simultaneously. My hand shook as I opened the door and looked up at the two broad-shouldered Navy officers, each with gold bands around their cuffs and multiple badges on their lapels.

My mouth went dry. "Yes? Can I help you?"

The slightly taller of the two, a man in his late forties perhaps, removed his black peak cap. "Miss, are you the sister of Able Seaman Roy Beckett?"

What am I going to tell Mum and Dad?

My throat clamped down on itself. "Yes?" I tried to keep breathing.

"I'm Lieutenant Ford, this is Lieutenant Warren. Miss, we believe Able Seaman Beckett has deserted," the other man said. "We know he was on leave not long ago. He was scheduled to depart yesterday morning and was not present at the time of departure and has not been seen or heard from for a few days."

I stared up at him, feeling only slightly relieved. "What?"

"We have reason to believe he is in hiding in London," Lieutenant Warren said. "As you probably know, desertion of war duties is a serious offense. When was the last time you spoke to your brother?"

"He was in London a few days ago, we traveled to Hazeldon together on the train and then he took the train to Southampton on Tuesday morning," I blurted. "There must be some mistake. Are you sure he didn't fall overboard or something?"

The two officers exchanged glances.

"Miss Beckett, did your brother say anything to you that might make you think he was planning to desert?"

"No, nothing—"

"Did he act strangely or say anything you found suspicious?"

"Um, I suppose he was reluctant to talk about his time on the ship but I think he only avoided it so my mother wouldn't worry too much." The pitch of my voice rose. "You think he just left? Roy wouldn't do that."

Lieutenant Ford glanced at the staircase behind me. "We would like to search the premises."

My eyebrows went up. "You think I'm hiding him here? I promise you, I'm not."

"Unfortunately we cannot simply take your word for it."

I swallowed. "Alright. If you insist." I moved to the side so they could carry out their duties. Following them upstairs, I heard Mrs.

Martin speak to one of them, sounding very irritated by the situation.

"If there was a young man hiding in my house, I would know about it!"

"We understand," Warren said. "However, Able Seaman Beckett is not the first man to flee from his war duties."

"You would be surprised where we have found some deserters trying to hide," Ford added.

"I know Mr. Beckett. He's a good boy," Mrs. Martin said. "He wouldn't simply run away."

As the two scoured the flat, Nora put her arm around me. "Are you alright?"

"It doesn't make any sense," I whispered. "They must be wrong about him being a deserter. I'm scared something has happened to him."

"Surely if something *did* happen to him, someone on the ship would have seen it. I would rather believe my brother was a deserter than, well…" she hesitated, "…something much worse."

The three of us followed the officers upstairs to the second floor of the flat, checking the bathroom and every bedroom. Ford stopped in the hall by the top of the staircase, eyeing a square in the ceiling with a little rope handle sticking out from the edge. I hadn't actually noticed it before.

Mrs. Martin saw his curious expression. "That's the hatch door to the attic. I haven't been up there in years. The ladder is too steep for me."

Ford stretched to reach the handle, pulling the hatch open and sliding the ladder down with it.

"There's nothing up there," Mrs. Martin warned as he climbed the ladder.

"Did you check under my pillow?" I heard Nora say from her bedroom doorway as she watched Lieutenant Warren poke around her things.

"How about the little drawer in my sewing machine?" She smirked. "Not under my bed? Oh, that's a shame. Excuse me, I would ask you to not look in my underwear drawer, sir!"

He scowled at her as he left the room. Nora pursed her lips and crossed her arms over her chest. "Prig," she muttered under her breath. "I'm going to be late for work."

She disappeared behind her bedroom door and the two men reconvened, comparing notes in a hushed tone.

"Are you about done here, officers?" Mrs. Martin gestured to the stairs. "Or should I make us all some tea if you're going to be here all day?"

Ford scowled. "Do you own the shop downstairs as well?"

"My brother owns it with his friend and I work there," I cut in. "He's not there either but you're welcome to search the shop if you want."

If Roy is *there, I'll kill him before they can arrest him.*

I followed Ford and Warren back downstairs and unlocked the shop for them so they could continue their search. I showed them the photography development room and the storage room where Cal and I slept that night during a raid. They even had me unlock Cal's office.

Ford handed me a slip of paper featuring his contact information. "Please let us know if you hear from your brother or if you have any idea where he might be hiding."

"I stand by what I said before," I said, my voice wavering. "I think you've made a mistake."

Trying to calm my nerves and regain some sense of normality, I took the blackout curtains down from the windows. Minutes later, Cal appeared on the other side of the window and smiled at me, cocking one brow when he found the front door still locked. In my preoccupied haze, I'd forgotten to unlock it.

He snickered as I let him in. "Trying to keep me out?"

"No, sorry." I laughed weakly. "Bit of an odd morning."

"How so?"

I folded the blackout curtain up and stowed it in the back. "Two Navy officers came by this morning."

When I came back out onto the shop floor, Cal's face was frozen, his blue eyes wide. It was then I noticed how bloodshot they looked.

"They believe Roy has deserted," I explained. "I told them that was impossible, that Roy would never do that. They didn't seem too interested in my thoughts though."

Cal swallowed, his shoulders rigid. "What else did they say?"

"Not much. They searched the flat upstairs, all over, and then down here and in the cellar too," I said. "They think he's somewhere in London."

"Why do they think he's in London?"

"They didn't say." I sighed and faced the window, watching the early morning shoppers hurry by. "I'm so worried something terrible has happened to him, Cal. What if he went overboard?" I looked at him over my shoulder as a terrible ache gripped my throat.

"If that was the case, surely someone would have seen it—"

I turned around, studying his expression. "You think he really has deserted, don't you?" My voice was shaky as I uttered the question.

Cal cast his gaze to a nearby shelf. "I don't know what I think. It's such a shock." He looked back at me. "If he has deserted… it's not something I would expect of him, no."

"He didn't say anything unusual to you before he and I took the train to Hazeldon?"

He shook his head.

Wiping at a stray tear rolling down my cheek, I sniffed. "How am I going to tell our parents?"

"I expect those Navy officers will probably check your parents' house next, so you probably won't get the chance to tell them anything."

"This stupid war." I sniffed again as a second tear escaped. "If Roy really has deserted and made us all worry about him, I'm going to be so mad at him." I took a deep breath and released it slowly, my chest quivering.

Suddenly Cal's arms were around me. I buried my face into the fibers of his knit jumper, the natural smells of the wool soothing me. His warm cheek rested on top of my head, his palm slowly and tenderly rubbing the middle of my back. I looked up at him, his arms still enveloping me.

His eyes searched mine, revealing a yearning that made the heat rise in my face. But I couldn't look away. I couldn't pull away from him. I didn't want to.

As confusing as it was, I *liked* the way Cal was looking at me—like

I was the only thing that mattered in that moment. My stomach tingled as he touched his forehead to mine.

And then the bell above the door chimed, Cal's arms dropped to his sides, and I slipped past him to escape to the back room in a blink.

As I shut the back room door I heard Cal apologizing to a customer.

"Sorry about that. My coworker got some unfortunate news about a loved one," he said. "Is there anything I can help you with this morning?"

Hearing bad news about a family member was so common in those days that everyone understood exactly what that meant: the war. It could mean someone was missing, injured, or dead. The customer didn't seem too bothered by it. I'm sure I wasn't the first shop girl to be weepy on the job, and I wouldn't be the last.

Of course they'd also seen us embracing. That wasn't *just* a comforting hug between friends. I wasn't exactly sure what it was.

He would have kissed me. Cal Woodbury wanted to kiss me.

I leaned against the wall and took a few deep breaths, trying to calm the buzzing in my abdomen.

What happens now?

I wasn't sure if we were supposed to talk about what happened or if we went on with our day like nothing occurred between us. But more importantly…

What would kissing Cal Woodbury be like?

Not that it would have been the first time we kissed but I was pretty sure the kiss we shared in the Hazeldon woods as children didn't really count.

I shook my head, attempting to vanquish the thought. Cal was my brother's best friend. I knew Roy didn't want anything happening between Cal and I—he was clear on that.

That knowledge, however, didn't chase away the visions of us together in my mind or calm the frantic pounding of my heart.

When I came back from my lunch break later on that day, Cal was rubbing his eyes with his index finger and thumb.

"Rough night?" I smiled at him. "Shall I make us some tea?"

He nodded and plucked the pencil from behind his ear. "Thank you, yes."

A few customers filed in as I filled the kettle in the small lavatory opposite the office and prepared our tea in the tiny makeshift kitchen. Cal had been rubbing his eyes all day. I wondered if the bombs bothered him more than usual the night before or if something else affected his sleep.

While I waited for the kettle to boil my mind wandered off somewhere. Suddenly I was in Cal's flat—a place I had never been, mind you—with the two of us laying on his bed, his tall and fit form molding around mine, his exceptional arms around my middle, pulling me close. In this daydream, he brushed my hair away so he could lay a delicate kiss on my neck. I watched as he worked the buttons of my blouse before sliding his hand beneath the fabric, his fingertips brushing my warm, bare flesh. I peeled his shirt from his body, yanking it roughly over his head, our mouths finally merging in a desperate clash of lips, tongues, and longing.

The whistling of the kettle brought me back to the real world. Fantasy or not, my cheeks burned.

It was far from the first time I had fantasized about Cal but never during work hours before. Those thoughts were saved for when I was in my bed in the wee hours of the morning after the all-clear siren had gone.

Cal was finishing up with the customers when I returned to the shop floor with our tea. He blinked hard as he lifted his cup to his lips.

"Why don't you go home and get some sleep? You look exhausted."

Cal smiled weakly, albeit very briefly. His eyes unfocused. He dropped his cup. Most of the hot tea splashed onto his shoes and on the bottom of his trousers. The cup broke into two pieces with a loud crack.

I stared at him. "Cal, what's wrong? Are you alright?" I put my tea on the counter.

He didn't respond. He kept staring into the middle distance, his expression blank. His left shoulder gave a tiny twitch—so tiny I likely would have missed it if I hadn't been watching him so closely.

After a few seconds, he looked back at me. "Sorry, did you say something?"

"Your pants," I said. "You dropped your tea."

Again, he didn't respond. He *was* looking at me but at the same time, he wasn't looking at me at all. He was looking at nothing and I just happened to be in the way.

"Cal." I waved a hand in front of his face but it stayed still as stone. "Cal?"

After about ten of the scariest seconds of my life, he frowned at the floor. "Oh. My tea."

"You dropped it," I repeated, trying to sound much calmer than I felt. "Go have a seat in the office. I'll clean this up."

"I'm fine, I can get it—"

"You aren't well, go—"

"I said I'm fine," Cal snapped. He closed his eyes and he rubbed his eyes again. "Sorry." He exhaled and rushed to the back room, mumbling, "I'm sorry." under his breath.

I flipped the Open sign in the front window temporarily while I cleaned up the puddle of tea and the broken cup from the floor. I heard a door shut while I washed my hands in the lavatory. When I came back out the office was empty, but the lamp was left on. Sitting on the desk, bathed in the yellow radiance of the lamp, was a note written in Cal's tight, cramped hand.

Went home. I'm sorry. -Cal

fourteen

Cal

I probably shouldn't have left like I did. But if I was going to have a second—maybe third? I wasn't sure—seizure, I didn't want to be anywhere near Maisie when it occurred. The fear in her wide eyes and the shakiness in her voice were unbearable.

Fortunately, I made it home without blacking out again. My head began to throb, and I was still in a bit of a fog, nearly taking the wrong street on the way back to my flat.

As I struggled to get my key in the door, Roy whipped it open from inside and I almost jumped out of my skin. I'd forgotten he was there. He was grinning like an idiot with Tiger cradled like a baby in the crook of one arm.

I shoved him aside and quickly closed the door. "Someone could have seen you," I snarled, keeping my voice low.

He rolled his eyes and took a seat on the couch. Tiger wriggled away and climbed up Roy to get to the back of the couch where he stretched out and watched out the window.

"I see you and the kitten have become rather chummy," I said.

"We've been having fascinating conversations about world events,"

Roy said. "I am worried he's a little too radical when it comes to his thoughts on socialism though." His brow suddenly pinched. "Wait, why are you home?"

"Taking the rest of the day off." I took a seat at the other end of the couch. "I had a seizure, maybe two."

"In front of Maisie?"

I gave a stiff nod.

"Well," he said, standing again, "at least she knows why you're not serving in the war now. I mean, the real reason." He headed to the loo.

"Hmm?"

He poked his head out from the hallway. "I told her you have syphilis." And then he disappeared again, shutting the bathroom door.

That bastard.

About a minute later, there was a knock at the door. If I had been less disoriented, I may have stayed put and kept silent as Roy and I planned. But I answered the door like a bloody fool.

A Navy officer stood in the hallway. It must have been one of the officers that searched Maisie's flat earlier that day. Swallowing, I silently ordered Roy to stay where he was and keep quiet. I had no idea how they found out where I lived as Maisie hadn't mentioned giving out my address.

"I'm Lieutenant Ford," he said. "I'm looking for Able Seaman Roy Beckett. We believe he has deserted his duties and that you may have seen him recently."

"No, I haven't seen him." I shook my head. "Well, except for the other day when he came to the shop."

Lieutenant Ford took out a notepad and pencil and jotted a note. "Did he say anything unusual at that time?"

I pretended to try to remember. "No. No, not that I remember."

He took a quick glance inside the flat behind me. "Would you mind if we took a look around your flat?"

I wanted to vomit.

Opening the door wider, I moved aside. I began considering how my mother would react to the news of my impending incarceration and if Maisie would visit me in prison.

As Ford slowly moved from living room to kitchen, I tried to remember where Roy's things were. His duffle bag was stashed under the couch, his shoes were next to the door but we were about the same size so I could say they were mine. Roy's toothbrush was in the bathroom but, well, so was Roy for that matter.

I could hear my pulse pumping in my ears.

"Do you live alone?" He glanced into the sink.

Multiple plates. Multiple forks and cups.

"Yes, sir."

"Another officer is checking Beckett's parents' home in Hazeldon to see if he's been there," he said, "but we have reason to believe he's in London."

"Why do you think that?"

"That's classified."

"Right." I smiled weakly.

He checked the bedroom next, peering under my bed and checking to make sure the wardrobe held clothing and not a runaway sailor.

The only other place to look was in the loo.

"Is this the privy? Why is the door closed?"

"Upset stomach," I blurted. "That's why I came home early from work."

As I regretted my words and every decision I made in my life up to that point, Lieutenant Ford raised an eyebrow at me as he reached for the doorknob.

"Don't," I said and then immediately wished I hadn't.

Ford frowned at me and opened the door, scanning the room. He took a step inside.

I held my breath, my whole body clenching. I wondered if I should make a run for it and live the rest of my days as an outlaw.

The shower curtain rustled loudly as it was yanked aside. Clenching, I waited for the shouting to begin.

He's not there. How is that possible?

The tension in my shoulders relaxed a little. I heard the scratching of a pencil on paper and the ripping of a page. I exhaled.

Ford returned to the hall and handed me a piece of paper with his contact information on it. "Please let me know if you see or hear from your friend. Thank you for your time."

"Yes, sir," I said, staring at the paper scrap. "Of course."

I closed the door behind him, waited a moment and then let out a long sigh, relief flooding my body. Rushing to the bathroom, I stepped into the tub, threw the window open further than the inch it was already cracked, and poked my head out.

Balancing precariously on a nearby window frame, Roy looked up at me, his chest heaving. His white-knuckled hands were gripping the iron bars of a balconet, and he was likely one strong gust of wind away from certain death. He grabbed my hand. I clung to his arm and hauled him back inside through the window. He toppled into the tub, gulping air and resting his forehead against the porcelain edge.

I leaned against the wall opposite, catching my breath. "Do you think anyone saw you?"

He shook his head. "Or if they did, they didn't shout at me or anything."

"That was close. That was too close."

I opened my mouth to tell him he needed to leave but Roy spoke first.

"Thank you for covering for me," he said. "You're a lifesaver."

I glared at the tub, my jaw clenched. "You're welcome."

The following day I arrived at the shop and, like usual, Maisie was already there. Except this time she wore a smile that didn't quite reach her eyes.

I knew that smile. I hated that smile. It was the fake smile my first girlfriend gave me while telling me she met someone else. It was the fake smile my grandmother gave me when her mind was going and she only pretended to know who I was. It was the fake smile my father gave me as he told me he was leaving Mum but that we would still see each other all the time.

"Good morning," she said. "Would you like me to make us some tea?"

I lowered my eyes and headed for the back room. "I can make my own tea, thanks."

"Oh, okay." Her voice was so small. I wanted to punch myself for being such a prat.

Peering back out at her, I asked, "Would you like me to make you some tea?"

"I had some, thank you."

There it was again. The smile.

I was grateful when a few customers came in as I returned to the shop floor so Maisie couldn't ask me any questions. I worked in my ledger in the office and wrote a few letters to distributors as she tended to the customers. We were running low on so many items because our distributors simply couldn't get them. Binoculars were impossible to get and paint was becoming scarce. Almost everything made out of metal was simply gone. Even some types of paper were now considered precious commodities—far too precious to be squandered on a hobby.

One of our regular toy manufacturers converted their facility to a munitions factory. Customers were becoming more tight-fisted with their money by the day and for good reason. I wanted to have at least *some* items available in the shop for Christmas, but at this rate I wasn't sure how to go about doing that. It wasn't yet mid-October.

Once the store was free of customers, Maisie leaned against the doorway to the back room.

"Do you want to talk about what happened yesterday?"

"No, not especially." I kept my head down.

She paused a long while. "Do they happen often?"

I looked at her over my shoulder and frowned.

"I only ask," she said, "so I can know what to do if they happen again."

"You don't need to do anything." I shrugged. "Just let me know what I missed." I turned back to my ledger. "They only happen when I'm especially tired."

"Okay," she said firmly. "That's all I need to know."

"Grand," I mumbled. "By the way, your friend Lieutenant Ford stopped by yesterday afternoon after I arrived home."

"Oh?"

"Your parents also likely had a visit from an officer yesterday too."

She sighed. "I bet my mum let him have it for suggesting her boy would do such a thing."

I stopped and turned around in my seat to face her. "If it's true, if he really has deserted, will you be angry with him?"

Maisie considered for a moment. "I don't know. I've been thinking about it for a day now and I still don't know. What about you?"

Our eyes locked and I nearly collapsed in on myself. I felt my resolve crumbling as I looked at those beautiful brown eyes and that porcelain doll face.

"I think Roy, if he did desert, must have his reasons," I said carefully. "It might be something you or I will never understand."

Maisie raised an eyebrow at this and opened her mouth to respond but the front door opened first. She closed the door to the back room and left me alone with my paperwork.

Running a hand through my hair, I grabbed a fistful of it in the back and yanked it, groaning quietly to myself.

I loathed having to maneuver my words around lying to Maisie. She was so pure and perfect that it felt entirely criminal.

Criminal. That's what I was now. A criminal hiding a fellow criminal.

Roy was right though—Maisie couldn't know. She couldn't be involved in our scheme to protect him from the authorities. I had no choice but to lie, no matter how much it killed me to do so.

fifteen

Maisie

"You better make me look good in these pictures," Louise said, glancing at me over her shoulder as she climbed the ladder into the attic. "Nobody told me I'd have to get up early on a Sunday morning."

"Forget looking good," Gladys said from inside the attic hatch at the top of the ladder. "I want to look divine."

Smiling weakly, I followed Louise up the ladder. "I'll do my best."

"Don't worry, girls," Nora added from the bottom of the ladder, waiting for me to complete my ascent. "You'll look the bee's knees in your photos. Your boyfriends won't even *think* of another bird when they see these photos."

Gladys frowned at me as I scooted up inside the attic. "Oh. I'd never have *that* problem. My bloke knows I'd kill 'im if he even *thought* about two-timing."

Nora and I slowly exchanged looks as she pulled herself up into the attic. She shrugged and pulled the ladder up so if Mrs. Martin happened to arrive home from church early and come upstairs, she might not realize right away we were in the attic.

Nora and I spent hours lugging photography lights from the hobby shop basement up to the attic, setting them up and practicing poses.

While Nora worked on Gladys' makeup on a nearby stool, Louise got changed behind the sheet we'd hung up in the corner. She'd come over with her makeup done already.

"What's that?" Gladys pointed to the little bowl Nora held as she brushed the homemade concoction on Gladys' eyelashes. "I haven't been able to find mascara in any of the shops for a month."

"Burnt cork and Vaseline. Stay still."

I put a Benny Goodman record on to help get the girls in the right mood and Louise peered out from behind the sheet, her lovely golden curls framing her angelic face.

"Well, come on, Lou," Gladys urged. "Let's see it!"

Louise bit the corner of her lip and shyly slid out from behind the curtain. The girl may have been all legs but I could tell she was getting cold feet.

"You look *gorgeous*," I said, getting my camera ready.

"Maisie, I didn't know you were photographing Betty Grable today," Nora added with a grin.

"Beautiful!" Gladys added.

Louise beamed. "Alright, let's do this before I change my mind." She tugged at the bottom edges of the short white dress Nora made for her.

When Nora and I first realized the attic would make a perfect photography studio, we spent hours pushing all the boxes of junk to the far end of the attic. We considered throwing a sheet over some creatively positioned boxes and using that as a backdrop for our models. However, while cleaning, we discovered a stunning blue velvet chair with ornate details on the arms. There was a rather large chunk missing from one arm, but we figured if we positioned the chair at an angle and put a cushion on that side it wouldn't even be noticeable. Once we cleaned the dust off it, the whole setup looked rather chic.

Louise positioned herself on the edge of the chair with her back straight as a pin and smiled at the camera like she was sitting for a royal portrait. I would need to get her to relax.

"Tell me about your boyfriend," I suggested, doing a quick lighting adjustment. "What's he like?"

She seemed surprised. "Well, uh, he's very sweet to me. Alfred is a bit of a shy guy, but he really opens up when it's just the two of us. People don't believe me when I say he's the funniest person I know." Her eyes glowed with love and her face softened as she thought about her fellow, and I grabbed a couple shots.

"How did the two of you meet?"

"Oh, we've known each other forever. He's a friend of my brother's so I was off limits for a long time," she said with a smirk.

I thought of Cal and Roy's longtime friendship and wondered if Roy told Cal he wasn't allowed to date me. Knowing Roy, he probably had.

"But one night we were all out together with a bunch of friends," she continued, "and I said to him, I said, 'Al, if you don't ask me to dance right now, I'll pour this pint right in your lap." She laughed and I snapped like mad. Her wide, laughing smile was so fun and genuine. "We've been together ever since."

"Can I get you to tilt your chin up a little? And relax your shoulders a bit," I coached gently.

She did as I suggested and my camera went click-click-click. Nora stood by my side as Gladys changed into her outfit behind the sheet.

"What is Al's favorite part of you?" Nora said. "I'm sure he loves how smart and charming you are but every bloke has that one thing—"

"My legs," Louise said, chuckling. "He loves my long legs."

Nora gave a business-like nod. "Right." She quickly moved around to Louise's side. "Try swinging around sideways in the chair with your legs over the arm? Yes, just like that. Do you mind if I make a few adjustments?"

Louise nodded encouragingly, and Nora brushed aside a few hairs, positioned Louise's legs so they were the co-stars of the next shot. She also pushed up the hem of her dress so the camera captured the entire stocking, in addition to a glimpse of bare thigh above that.

Louise giggled and the next few photos were some of my favorites from that session—she looked like a mischievous little vixen.

"Hold that pose for a second," I said before whispering a styling suggestion to Nora.

She nodded and quickly unbuckled one of Louise's shoes so it was dangling off her foot without quite falling off.

That was it. That was *the* shot.

Gladys wasn't shy like Louise, not even for a second. A silky peach bathing costume hit her hourglass frame perfectly and, more importantly, she obviously felt attractive in it as well. It was quickly clear her goal wasn't only to keep her boyfriend—it was also to outdo Louise in the posing department as well.

While angelic Louise smiled and giggled, dark-haired Gladys went for more of a dramatic, serious tone, smiling with her eyes alone and pouting her full lips. The winning pose, however, was when she let her head fall back and let slip a subtle smirk at the camera, one sassy eyebrow arched.

"Perfect," I said, snapping away.

"She's not showing too much thigh, is she?" Nora bit her lip beside me. "I don't want anyone to get in trouble."

Gladys peeked down at the underside of her bare, bent leg. "Oh, it's fine. Besides, my lad'll love it."

After the photo session, the girls got changed in a rush since Mrs. Martin was due home soon. Louise left the white dress on the chair since she had only "rented" it and we could use it for future clients.

"Now, I know I mentioned this before, but it's really important you don't share our names with anyone," Nora warned Louise and Gladys. "Feel free to tell your friends but please let them know it's a bit of a risky venture. Let's maybe stick with first names only. Not everyone appreciates a bit o' thigh showing, you know what I mean?"

"If you tell your friends about this, make sure they know they absolutely *cannot* show up unannounced at our address," I added. "Our landlady must not find out and neither can the bloke who owns the shop. We need to keep this hush-hush, alright?"

The girls nodded, happily handed over the session fee, and Nora lowered the ladder for them. She showed them out while I shut off all the lights in the attic and put the hatch back into place. Mrs. Martin would have no idea we had even been up there.

Nora, eyes sparkling, found me in my bedroom and leaned against the doorframe.

"That was so much fun," she said with a bit of a squeal at the end. "Honestly, I would do that for free."

"I would definitely do that again," I said. "The money is too good to just say no to."

"I'm glad to hear you say that," Nora said, hesitating. "Because four friends of friends have already asked for photo sessions too."

I blew out a breath and puffed out my cheeks. "Oh, wow. I guess I better hurry up and develop today's photos then."

Nora beamed. "You seemed very comfortable and you looked like you were having fun."

"I did." A smile spread across my face. "I was surprised how easily everything my aunt taught me came back so quickly."

"Do you think she would approve of the type of photography we're doing?'

I laughed. "Aunt Jean? Oh, yes. If anything, she would be jealous." I shrugged. "But she would approve no matter what, as long as I was enjoying myself. Now, my parents, that's a different story."

"What about Cal?" Nora arched an eyebrow.

Cringing, I frowned. "I don't think he would be delighted that I was using the shop's dark room for developing and the shop's chemicals and film and—"

"You're not taking your full shop wages. The shop *owes* you." She waved a hand at me. "I don't know Cal very well, but I can't see him being a prig about it." Nora's lips puckered as she tried to restrain a grin. "I think he would want one of those photos of *you* for himself."

"Oh, stop," I said with a laugh. "I'm just his friend's sister to him, that's all."

"Of course you are," she said with a wink.

I hadn't told Nora about Cal's seizures or how he acted so closed off ever since. I really hoped his discomfort wouldn't last.

I also hadn't mentioned how Cal embraced me and how I *thought* that just *maybe* he wanted to kiss me. And I hadn't told her how much I wanted him to kiss me. And I *definitely* hadn't told her how often I'd been thinking about that moment ever since.

All. The. Time.

sixteen

Cal

It was an especially rough week for jolly old London. It would later be known as one of the most tragic weeks of the entire Blitz.

Francis and Jack, two of my mates from the cleanup crew, sat across the booth from me at the pub close to the shop. They'd invited me out for drinks and Maisie wanted to see a movie with her friend Nora so we agreed to shut the shop a little early.

Jack and Francis both lost someone that week. Francis' cousin was one of the sixty-eight poor souls who drowned while sheltering at Balham station and one of Jack's school chums was killed when a bomb took out an entire block of flats in Hackney and everything collapsed into the shelter below, taking the lives of at least 150 people.

The least I could do was share a drink with them.

Besides, I needed a break from Roy. Always an extrovert, he was nearly going mad from being inside my flat all day, every day. At least I could grab something to eat at the pub while out with friends. My appetite was not a huge supporter of splitting my ration book between the two of us.

"This goddamn war," Francis said before downing the rest of

his pint.

Jack sat back against the wooden booth seats. He raised an eyebrow as he studied me. "Why aren't you serving anyway?"

"Why aren't you?"

He likely noticed we were nearly the only lads in the pub who were under the age of forty. What a difference to a Saturday night the war made.

"I'm a teacher." Jack shrugged. "Reserved occupation."

"Dockworkers are reserved too," Francis added. "I thought about quitting so I could sign up. I still might. I don't know." He eyed me. "Hobby shop owner, that's reserved too, eh?"

I gave an exaggerated nod. "Of course it is."

"I think I need another pint." Francis slid out of the booth. "And I think I need to go have a chat with that lovely creature behind the bar." As he got up, something caught his eye from the other side of the nearby window. "Oy, Cal, isn't that your girl?"

"What?" I glanced out the window to see Maisie and Nora walking towards the pub. "She's not *my* girl, she's just *a* girl—"

"Jack, give the window a knock," Francis ordered. "Get their attention, will ya?"

"Don't—" I threw Jack a glare as he gave the window a hard rap.

Both the girls turned. Maisie's face lit up as she saw me, her thick chocolate curls bouncing against her red scarf as she turned.

Nora, meanwhile, looked confused, her face softening when she recognized me.

I smiled shyly at Maisie and looked down at my beer and chips, expecting the ladies to keep walking. But when I looked up again, they were at the door and then sliding into the booth with us. As Francis disappeared to go woo the landlord's daughter, Nora slid in beside Jack and Maisie took the available spot next to me.

"Hello stranger," she said, plucking one of my chips from the plate and taking a bite.

"Hi," I said.

Seeing her outside the shop felt so odd. We spent all week together but then seeing her outside of work hours felt like a treat. She was ice cream on a hot day. She was hot cocoa in a snowstorm. I wanted to devour her.

But she felt so beyond my reach.

Removing her black beret, she ran her fingers through her hair and shrugged off her coat.

Her friend gave me a friendly smile before offering a handshake to Jack. "I'm Nora."

"Jack." He shook her hand and tilted his head slightly. "Do I know you from somewhere?"

"Do you?" Her eyes narrowed. "Maybe?"

Maisie slowly looked back at me with a knowing expression and then leaned in closer to me. "Do you think they know each other or is that a line Jack uses on women?"

"It's hard to tell," I said, my lips so close to her ear a strand of her hair fell across my nose.

She tucked the hair away behind her ear and reached for another chip.

"I'm sorry," she said, pulling her hand back. "I didn't get a chance to eat anything before we went to the cinema."

I shrugged and slid the plate closer to her. "How was the movie?"

She popped a small crispy chip into her mouth. "Fantastic."

Jack piped up. "I'm off to the bar. Would you ladies like a drink?"

"I'll have a half-pint of lager," Nora said, sliding out of the booth so Jack could squeeze by. "Maisie, you're having a drink too, right?" She tilted her chin down and lifted her eyebrow in a less-than-subtle gesture.

"I'll have a sherry if they have it," she said. "Thank you."

Nora returned to her spot. "How is Tiger?"

I chuckled. "He's a troublemaker. He was very happy to get his cast off last week."

"You're going to keep him, right?" Maisie looked up at me through long dark eyelashes.

"I think so," I said. "I might see if my cousins want a kitten. If my uncle would allow it, of course."

A moment later Jack returned with the drinks. He slid a golden glass my way.

"Thanks," I said with a nod before taking a massive gulp of

liquid courage.

As we drank, Maisie and I mostly chatted between the two of us, chiefly about silly things we did as children. I shared a few funny stories about my adolescent years when Mum and I lived with my uncle, aunt, and cousins. We both managed to avoid bringing up the shop *and* her brother. Jack and Nora across from us were openly flirting and I was envious at how easy it came to both of them.

I did have to wonder, though, if Maisie smiled at anyone else the way she smiled at me that evening.

Someone turned the wireless up and the sounds of chatter, laughter, and glasses clinking was drowned out slightly by a cheerful big band number. Francis was leading some pretty thing—noticeably, not the same girl as earlier—out to one of the only bare patches of space in the place and twirling her around with ease.

Nora pursed her lips at Jack. "Aren't you going to ask me to dance?"

He finished his drink, slid out of the booth and offered his hand. She gladly took it and they joined Francis and his gal.

I took another swig of beer as Maisie gave me an expectant look.

"I'm rubbish at dancing," I said with a quiet chuckle, rubbing the back of my neck.

She rolled her eyes, grabbed my hand and dragged me out of the booth as the song switched from something bouncy to a romantic song *everybody* knew—Glenn Miller's "Moonlight Serenade."

Maisie and I looked at one another and I laughed awkwardly as she placed her hand into mine and I put my other hand on her lower back. My heart raced as she slid her other hand onto my shoulder and we began to sway to the melody. There wasn't much room for dancing in the crowded pub, so we were squeezed together so closely I could feel the warmth of her breath on my neck. I was fascinated by how small and soft her hand seemed, cradled in mine. She gave me a quick, soft smile before resting her head on my chest, sending my pulse skyrocketing.

I knew in that moment specifically that there was no going back for me. I was a goner.

Francis and his girl, a WVS volunteer going by her uniform, looked quite cozy as they danced nearby. As for Nora and Jack, well, they disappeared entirely.

As the song changed, I leaned in to whisper to Maisie, "I think your friend left with my friend." I was in no hurry to let go of her.

She glanced around frantically, her hand leaving my shoulder. "Oh. Actually, what time is it?" Maisie squinted at the clock on the wall by the door. "I should probably get home."

"Right." I nodded, resigned.

"Tonight was fun," she said before glancing at our hands, still clasped together between us.

I immediately pulled my hand away. "Sorry." I shook my head.

Idiot. Could you be more obvious?

"It's alright," she said. "I don't mind."

She slipped through the pub to fetch her coat, hat, and scarf before I could blurt out anything stupid. I followed, her words echoing in my ears.

"I don't mind."? What does that mean? That's got to mean something.

"Let me walk you home," I said, quickly adding, "I'm going that direction anyway."

I grabbed my coat and cap, threw some random bills on the table—I'm certain I over-tipped by an absurd amount—and Maisie and I escaped into the cool evening street.

I stuffed my hands into my pockets to protect them from the chill in the air. The pub wasn't far from the shop and her flat above it so our walk was brief, even with us having to stop and make sure we were going down the right street in the dark.

When we reached the doorway, she smiled sweetly at me. "Thank you for walking me home."

I tore my eyes away from her mouth. "You're welcome."

In two short, hesitant steps, she closed the space between us, stood on tiptoe and kissed me on the cheek. Her lips were so soft—softer than I could ever imagine.

And I had spent a great deal of time imagining what those lips would feel like.

Her face lingered near mine and her nose brushed my skin, just above where she kissed a moment before. She looked up at me through thick eyelashes once more.

It happened so fast. All the various fantasies I'd had about Maisie in the last month and a half bonded together and put my body into motion.

Wrapping my arms around her swiftly and pulling her firmly against my chest, I pressed my lips to hers and poured every bit of want I had for her into that kiss. The feeling of her fingers gripping my back, the fruity taste of her mouth, the floral smell of her skin, and the delicate sound of her quiet, little sigh drove me absolutely mad. As the kiss deepened and I drew her in even closer to me, my blood raced and my heart hammered.

The air raid siren wailed, breaking the magic spell.

Our lips stayed locked in place for a moment as we both froze. Maisie slowly pulled her lips away and gave a little giggle as we separated.

"I'm sorry," I blurted. "I shouldn't have—"

She laughed gently again. "It's alright—"

"I should go—"

"Why don't you come to the Anderson shelter?"

"Because Mrs. Martin doesn't like me."

Maisie laughed louder. "Mrs. Martin doesn't like anyone."

I chuckled and felt the tension in my shoulders release a little. "There's a shelter close by. I should go." I wished it wasn't so damn dark so I could see her beautiful face a little better. "Good night, Maisie."

"Good night, Cal."

I heard her unlock the door, her keys jingling, as I made my way down the street.

A few minutes later, as I sat on a bench between an intoxicated man and a woman holding a screaming baby, I couldn't help but smile, my lips still tingling.

When the bombs began to drop above London soon after, I remembered the promise I'd made to Roy and all the joy evaporated.

seventeen

Maisie

"He kissed you!"

"Nora," I warned, putting a finger to my lips as Mrs. Martin was in the kitchen nearby.

"Sorry," Nora whispered, barely tamping down her giddiness. "What kind of kiss was it? Was it a peck or a proper grown-up kiss?"

"I'm not telling you *that*." I adjusted my sitting position on the couch in the living room and smirked at Nora. "Especially when you're not telling me what happened last night with you and Jack. The song ended and you were gone!"

The corner of Nora's mouth curled up and her eyes appeared even more cat-like than usual. "I told you, we went for a walk—"

"In the dark," I added.

"—and we took a wrong turn and ended up having to spend the night at the Blackfriars underground station shelter."

"And how was that?"

"The shelter? Rotten. The bombs overhead? Loud."

I narrowed my eyes at her. "And you didn't do any canoodling of your own?"

Nora pursed her lips. "We're talking about you right now, not me."

Sighing, I considered how much to share. "It was quite nice."

She nodded in silent understanding and picked up her knitting from her lap.

Nora didn't need to know how that passionate kiss made my entire body burn.

"When are you seeing him again? Outside of the shop, I mean."

"That's the thing," I said, frowning. "He didn't suggest we go on a date at all. We said goodnight and parted ways."

I didn't know if it was his shyness or if it was something else that stopped him.

Nora put her knitting down again and tented her fingers like some sort of professor, specializing in the mysteries of men. "I wonder if you should ask *him* instead of waiting for him to ask."

I scoffed. "Don't be absurd."

"I'm not being absurd at all! It's 1940, after all. Women are running the world while the boys are away." She shrugged. "It's a whole new dynamic."

I sighed and watched the rain hitting the windows behind the couch.

"Cal obviously adores you." She tapped a knitting needle against her cheek. "Is there a chance your brother told him he wasn't *allowed* to date you?"

"Almost certainly," I said. "However, Roy is missing so he wouldn't even know about it anyway."

But I knew Nora could be correct. Maybe Cal *was* just holding on to a promise from my needlessly overprotective brother.

I needed to know.

We lived in very uncertain times. Lives were lost every single night in London and you never knew if the next bomb might land on your neighbor's flat or the shop across the street. A person never knew when the next bomb might come for them.

"I would feel so odd asking him while we were at the shop," I said. "Maybe I should go to his flat and ask him."

Nora's eyes lit up. "Now?"

My stomach rolled at the thought. "I don't know. Should I?"

She rushed to put her knitting aside, grabbed my hand, and pulled me from the couch. "We're going to do your makeup and put you in something pretty."

With my curls neatened and mascara and lipstick applied, I took a moment to stop in front of Cal's building. I'd never been there before but I was pretty sure I had the right address. It was a lovely Georgian building in Holborn, all straight lines and neat rows of identical windows.

My heart pounded hard in my chest.

I had already stopped, turned around to go home, and then turned around again to continue towards his place at least five times during the short walk to his building. As I let myself into the downstairs entry, all of my doubts came creeping back to me, scraping their fingernails over my skin as I climbed the stairs to his floor.

He has feelings for me. I know he does.

After all, the kiss hadn't just been a drunken smooch. We hadn't even *had* that much to drink and it certainly felt significant at the time.

But what if it's all in my head? What if I only want for it to mean something?

In no time at all I stood in front of his door. It looked like any other wooden door, really. But most doors didn't have the capacity to make me feel half ill with nerves.

My toes felt crowded together in the fashionable heels Nora suggested I wear and the fabric of the floral dress she loaned me was beginning to make me sweat. Maybe it was the coat I wore over it. Actually, it wasn't the dress or the coat at all. It was just me.

I can still run right now.

If I put my ear close to the door, I could hear the low murmur of male voices inside—he was listening to the wireless, I assumed.

With a shaky fist, I knocked on the door quickly. I bit the inside of my lip as I waited for him to come to the door, all the while still considering making a dash for it.

The door opened only a couple inches, Cal's surprised face appearing inside the narrow frame.

"Hello," he said, unsmiling. "Is something wrong?"

"No," I said with a small chuckle. "No, nothing is wrong. I just, um, I wondered if we could, um, perhaps, talk."

Cal's brow pinched together as he swallowed. "Right, of course." Instead of opening the door so I could come in, he squeezed himself out of the narrow space and shut the door behind him.

I raised an eyebrow at him. "Oh, um, alright." I cast a glance over my shoulder, wondering how many of his neighbors were listening to us in the hallway.

"Sorry," he said, nodding to his door. "It's…a mess in there right now."

I thought of his desk in the office at the shop.

"That's alright," I said.

But instead of opening the door and letting us in, he nodded and waited for me to say my piece.

It was not like how I'd imagined it going at all.

My eyes narrowed slightly before a cold shock ran through me.

He has a girl in there.

"What was it you wanted to discuss?" He slid his hands into his pockets and studied the hallway carpet, rather than looking at me.

I blinked at him a few times, wondering if he could possibly be joking. I arched a brow. "What happened last night."

Obviously.

"Yes, right, of course." Cal rubbed the back of his neck. "Perhaps we should talk on Tuesday."

"Oh. Um, okay." My chest began to ache, and my throat tightened. "Of course."

The details of the walk back to Covent Garden were vague at best. Cal said my name as I walked away from him but didn't come after me. I stopped to wipe the tears from my eyes on the pavement outside his building. Everything else was a blur.

Before I reached Barnaby Street, I found a bench and sat to take several deep breaths. I needed to stop crying before I got to the flat or else Nora would go and confront Cal herself. She was a top shelf pal that way.

I was fairly certain he had a girl in his flat. Maybe he'd had a secret girlfriend the entire time and never told me because he wanted to mess me about.

If there was no girl in his flat, I thought, then he didn't want me in his private domain, pouring my heart out to him, only to tell me he didn't feel that way about me at all. In other words, Cal didn't want me weeping on his living room couch.

Either way, Cal lied to me, right to my face.

Dealing with my broken heart was one thing, but another question was now drumming in my mind.

How am I supposed to face him at the shop on Tuesday?

eighteen

CAL

As soon as Maisie disappeared down the stairs at the end of the hall, I opened the door to my flat and found Roy standing on the other side, his jaw clenched and his arms crossed over his chest.

"Was that my sister?"

I could tell by his tone he already knew it was.

I rushed to close the door before he raised his voice further. "Would you keep your voice down? Do you *want* to get caught?"

"What did she mean by 'what happened last night'?" Fury flared in his eyes as he stared at me. "I told you—"

"Nothing happened," I snapped. "Will you calm down—"

"I asked you to do one thing, Cal. One thing," Roy said, his lip curling into a snarl. "And you couldn't even do that." He shook his head at me, nostrils flaring. "What did you do?"

"Nothing happened," I repeated. "Something happened with me and her friend and her friend must have sent Maisie to talk to me, that's all."

Roy stepped closer to me, inspecting my face at an uncomfortably close proximity. "You're a terrible liar, do you know that?"

"You don't know what you're talking about." I rolled my eyes.

As I went to move around him, Roy gave me a shove and my back hit the coat rack and it tumbled over, hitting the floor with a loud clang. I glared at him.

He shook his head at me. "You're a traitor. After all I've done for you—"

"Oh, *I'm* the traitor? That's a fine thing for a deserter to say."

The words barely left my lips when Roy gave me another shove and I pushed him much harder, sending him tripping back onto the couch.

Tiger fled into my bedroom in a blur of orange.

Roy rose to his feet. "You're not good enough for Maisie." He glowered at me, his chest heaving.

"I'm not doing this with you."

"'Cause you know you'd end up a bloody mess—"

"That's enough," I said sharply. "You need to go take a walk or something." I opened the door wide.

"I'm not supposed to ever leave the flat, remember?" His tone was mocking.

"Get out."

Roy gave a stiff nod and grabbed his duffle from behind the couch and his coat from the floor. He slipped his shoes on, tossed his bag over his shoulder and left without a word or a second glance.

I slammed the door shut, locked it, and righted the coat rack. Peering out the window, I saw him strut down the street with his long strides, keeping his face lowered.

My eyes narrowed, and I cursed under my breath as I realized Roy stole my cap.

Kneeling on the floor beside my bed, I tried to beckon Tiger out from the far corner with a bit of canned tuna. He wasn't having it.

Sitting on the floor by the bed, I rested my head on the quilt and thought about how the day had not gone to plan, not at all. Roy, I figured, would likely end up arrested before I saw him again. Maybe it was for the best he went out on his own instead of dragging me down with him.

As for Maisie, the thought of her eyes filling with tears as she faced me in the hallway was killing me. If Roy hadn't been on the other side of that door, of course I would have invited her in and, probably, kissed her until she went weak in the knees.

However, as Roy so kindly pointed out, he *had* done a lot for me over the years, including literally saving my life. He asked me not to get involved with his sister and I did exactly that.

Maybe he was right. Maybe I really was a bad friend and undeserving of Maisie's affections. Or anyone else's for that matter.

When I arrived at the shop on Tuesday at ten minutes past opening time, I was surprised to find the door locked. If I had been paying more attention instead of fretting over what I might say to Maisie when I saw her that morning, perhaps I would have noticed the Closed sign still hung on the door and the blackout curtains were still over the windows.

Letting myself in, a very still and heavy silence hung in the air. The shop hadn't felt that way since before Maisie began working with me. She simply being there brought a warmth and a light to the little shop I hadn't actually noticed.

Until it was gone, that is.

"Maisie?" I called, peeking into the back room behind the shop.

I checked the basement and the locked office too, just in case. Not a single Maisie to be found. It was unlike her to be late.

My eyes finally landed on a small scrap of paper on the floor of the office that I hadn't noticed before. Written in Maisie's elegant and loopy hand was a message:

Going home for a few days. Fire me if you want. I don't care. -M

I read it a few times to make sure I was comprehending her message. Letting out a sigh, I slumped into the office chair and considered the note again.

Skipping work to leave on a whim was very out of character for Maisie. There could only be one reason for her fleeing London so suddenly and leaving me a note like that.

She hates me that much.

I tucked the note into my pocket and trudged back out to the shop floor. It was so quiet without her there. As I took the blackout curtains down, glimpses of Maisie smiling at me over her shoulder from the stool appeared in my mind. As I made tea, images of her eyes sparkling over a teacup came to me, rubbing salt in the wound.

A little later that morning, several large parcels arrived in the mail. As I surveyed them suspiciously, the mailman raised an eyebrow at me.

"Is everything alright, sir?"

"Mmm," I said. "There should be six boxes, not three." I checked the return address as I began unwrapping one parcel's brown paper. "Are you sure there's nothing else for us?"

He shrugged, his clipboard in hand. "That's all I've got for you, sorry. Probably a shortage. Lots of shops are in the same boat, ya know."

He handed me the clipboard and I signed with a frown. "Of course. Thank you."

As I unwrapped everything and began logging the products inside the boxes in our inventory, my heart continued to sink as I realized how many items were missing from the order.

"This won't do," I said, rubbing the back of my neck.

The empty, silent shop did not reply.

My shoulders falling, I let out a long breath. I knew I would be lucky if the shop survived until the new year. I checked out my ledgers, did some quick math and seriously considered if firing Maisie would be the best decision after all—not because she hadn't shown up for work but because she would go back to Hazeldon and be safe from the German bombers that still came to London every night. Plus, going back to one employee at the shop made the most financial sense.

It wasn't the most romantic gesture in the world, but I wasn't really supposed to be doing those. Roy seemed pretty firm on that.

Not that I'd seen a trace of Roy Beckett since he'd left my flat a few days before. Running away to get far from me had suddenly become a Beckett family tradition.

I nodded to myself, feeling confident in my decision. I made a plan: if Maisie came back to the shop to work later in the week, I would tell her the shop simply couldn't afford to keep her on and advise her to return to Hazeldon. That was that.

Drumming my fingers on the counter, I wondered if she might

find that upsetting.

Perhaps I could send her a telegram instead or maybe get Nora to tell her for me.

No, no. I knew that wouldn't do either. My plan was for her own good, for *her* safety.

I doubted she would see my decision that way.

When I arrived at the shop on Friday morning, the door was already unlocked and the blackout curtains were down. Maisie stood behind the counter, absorbed in a distributor's product catalog like it was a fascinating read.

When she finally did look up she met my gaze with dead, empty eyes.

"Good morning," I mumbled to the floor. "Welcome back."

"Good morning," she said flatly.

"How was the trip home? How are your parents?"

She gave me a silent glare before lowering her eyes to the catalog again. "Concerned about my brother and unconcerned about me. So, the usual."

"Given the circumstances—"

"He deserted," she snapped. "I tried to tell myself before it was a misunderstanding but it's quite clear Roy did, in fact, abandon his duties."

"You're not worried about him now?"

Maisie looked at me directly. "Of course I am. Mum and Dad are still in denial though, no matter what I tell them."

I wondered if her parents even asked how she was doing. I wondered if either of them noticed how different she seemed or, perhaps, only I was getting to see this icy and angry version of Maisie.

She slid the catalog off to the side and straightened her shoulders. "I noticed we have several films that were dropped off earlier this week so I better go deal with those."

She rounded the counter and started for the back room.

"Maisie, wait," I blurted.

She waited for me to say something. "What? Is there something else I should be doing?" Her tone wasn't quite rude but more straightforward and impersonal, bordering on unfriendly.

I had to fire her. I knew I had to fire her, that it was the best option in several ways.

But I just…I couldn't.

I finally dragged my gaze up to meet hers. "Do you want to continue working here?"

Her hesitation in answering seemed to last for hours when in reality it was only a few seconds.

"Yes." She swallowed. "I'm sorry. I shouldn't have left without letting you know first—"

I shook my head and exhaled loudly. "I don't care about that."

Her face softened ever so slightly. "If you want me to stay, I'll stay." There was something challenging in her voice.

I took in the details of that face I adored so much and stepped closer to her. "I want you to stay."

Her eyes narrowed slightly. I've never wanted to hug someone so much as I did in that moment, but I didn't dare move any closer to her. If she had any trust in me left at all, the tiny bit that remained hung by a thread.

A few customers arrived then, signaled by the ringing of the bell above the door.

"I'll be downstairs," she said, already on her way.

Although busy with customers and shop business, my Maisie-filled thoughts distracted me. I wanted the shop to glow like it used to when she was there. I needed her to be happy again, even if that happiness didn't involve me.

nineteen

Maisie

Cal's eyebrows kneaded together as he read the headline from that day's newspaper in mid-November. "Coventry has been obliterated." He leaned against the shop counter and scanned for the pertinent details. "At least five hundred people dead. The city is just…not *there* anymore. It's gone."

I joined him to look at the photo of the devastating scene. "Oh, goodness. Those poor souls!"

Obviously London received more than its fair share of bombs since the Blitz began, but at least buildings and landmarks were still mostly recognizable. Going by the photo in the newspaper Coventry was a flattened field of debris. Even their lovely cathedral only had a few walls left standing.

"Bloody hell," Cal muttered, shaking his head at the picture.

I glanced at Cal as he continued scanning the article for numbers—how many hurt, how many buildings reduced to dust. People all over England measured their days by those types of numbers.

Cal and I returned to a fairly comfortable level of workplace camaraderie since the, um, misunderstanding between us the month before. There were still nights where Cal invaded my dreams and there were still times I would catch him looking at me from across the room. But we came to an unspoken agreement we were workmates and nothing more.

Since the shop was a little quiet that afternoon, I made myself busy downstairs developing photographs while Cal manned the shop floor. I was finishing up and heading back upstairs near the end of the day when the doorbell jingled and a customer came in. I cracked the door so I could listen in while I made myself my last cup of tea for the day.

"Good afternoon," Cal said. "How can I help you?"

It was nice to hear Cal finally greeting customers properly, rather than the cold and dismissive acknowledgement he used to provide.

"Hi there," a bubbly young woman replied. "What an adorable shop! I've never been here before."

"Well, thank you."

"I'm actually here because I'm raising money for the Spitfire Fund. My brothers are both pilots so it's a cause really near and dear to my heart," she prattled quickly. "Would you care to make a donation?"

"Oh, of course, sure."

I heard some coins clinking together as he dropped a few into her donation box.

"Thank you so much," she said. "You know, I bet you'd look topping in an RAF uniform."

My ears perked up.

"Uh, thanks," he said quietly. "Unfortunately I'm completely blind."

"Are you pulling my leg?"

He chuckled awkwardly. "Yeah."

She giggled like she'd never heard something so hilarious. I rolled my eyes.

"You're too funny," she exclaimed in a melodic, flirtatious voice. "Say, a bunch of my friends and I are going to a dance this weekend in Farringdon and my date canceled. Would you…be interested?"

"Uhh—"

"You probably have a girlfriend," she cut in. "I'm sorry, I shouldn't have asked."

"Uh, well, I don't, um, have a girlfriend but, uh, um, I—"

No girlfriend? Maybe there really was *no girl in his flat then.*

"Don't worry about it. It's fine. It's just so rare to find younger guys in London these days, you know? Thanks for the donation." I listened as she hurried out.

The kettle whistled and I finished preparing my tea before joining Cal on the shop floor.

"Did I miss anything?" I smiled at him as he counted up the receipts for the day.

"No, all quiet here," he said, focusing on the paper slips.

You liar.

A few days later I was in the attic with Nora and a couple of new photography clients we'd met through Gladys. Both were West End actresses, tremendously chic, and both were looking for updated headshots. As usual we had a big band record on to get our clients in a fun and playful mood but it was quickly clear these two had no problems getting comfortable around us.

"Would it be possible to do headshots for the both of us and a pinup style photo for me if we have time?" Ruth asked as Nora applied some rouge (beetroot juice) to the apples of Ruth's cheeks. "I think my boyfriend would love it."

I shrugged. "I can't see why not. We should have time."

I continued adjusting the lights so the angle was perfect for her fellow actress, Irene. She had a Katharine Hepburn look about her, all high cheekbones and expressive eyes. She looked into the camera like it was an ex-lover she had exactly no time for, deploying a stunning yet sassy smirk and an arched brow. For our last few photos, she switched it up and went for a smolder that could melt chocolate.

Ruth, freshly made up, was more of a blonde cherub with her round face, Cupid's bow lips, and large, round eyes. She specialized in comedic roles and her headshots played this up—she pursed her lips and widened her eyes so they somehow looked even larger.

Once we were sure we got some great options for her headshot, she quickly changed into a short polka dot dress and returned to the blue chair. The silly cherub grew up before my eyes. She sat on her knees and hiked the dress up to show off her stockings and ample thigh.

"You've done this before," I joked, the shutter clicking loudly.

"My man's a busy chap," Ruth said, twisting her body so she was in profile and only sideways glancing at the camera from underneath thick eyelashes. "I have to make sure he remembers me at the end of a long day."

Irene lit a cigarette. "Nice guy, but has a lot on his plate. He works for the MOI."

The Ministry of Information was the British government department for educating the public on wartime measures and safety, promoting volunteering and deciding which news we, the British public, were allowed to know.

"He'd be less busy if he'd leave his wife like he said he was going to," Ruth added casually, facing the camera again.

Nora and I exchanged glances.

Ruth relaxed in the velvet blue chair and looked up at me. "Am I allowed to… unbutton?" She pointed to the top couple of buttons on the front of her dress.

"If you want to and you're comfortable, go ahead," I said. "It's entirely up to you."

I wondered exactly how much trouble I could get into for taking that sort of photograph.

Ruth didn't hesitate, popping a few buttons on the snug dress, her ample cleavage on full display. I got the impression she already fully considered this before arriving at our studio that day.

"Hold on," I said, scampering around the camera to fix a lock of Ruth's hair, tucking it neatly into her blonde waves.

The shutter clicked, and I glanced over my shoulder at Nora, grinning at me from behind the camera.

"Oops," she said with a mischievous giggle.

"Hey," I laughed. "Don't waste film on me."

Once I was back behind the lens, Ruth posed and puckered her lips like a top tier coquette.

"We got some fantastic shots," I said, switching the warm lights off once we finished. "I think you'll both be pleased."

Irene slid her arms into her raincoat. "I have a few actress friends who might be interested in getting new headshots done too. I'll pass your name on. Do you only photograph women or do you do headshots for male actors—"

"Yes, we *do* work with actors as well," Nora blurted. "Handsome single actors specifically."

twenty

CAL

Francis took a long drag from his cigarette and forcefully blew the smoke out through his nose. "Lovely day."

With a wrinkled nose, I squinted up at the gray sky, cold drizzle dotting my face. "Oh, aye."

It was Monday morning and Francis and I were doing our part for the war effort, shifting rubble off the roadways and pavement. It was so early that the streets were still fairly quiet and only a few Londoners were dashing to work. The wreckage of the tall and narrow building behind us was previously a shoe shop with a flat upstairs, similar to the hobby shop. Glass, stone, and wood splinters littered the shelves, surrounding the remnants of a bed that had fallen through the ceiling. Mangled and dusty shoes were strewn from wall to wall—or, at least, where the walls used to be.

After cleaning up so many of these places over the last couple of months, I'd become numb to the sight of a gutted home. As long as there were no human remains inside, it didn't seem to matter. They were only objects, after all, but I knew their owners likely didn't see it that way.

"Once we're done here, we're supposed to clean up a place two streets over," Francis said. "Actually, why don't I finish up here and you get started over there?"

He gave me the address and I set out, my shovel in my empty wheelbarrow.

Next to the shoe shop was another building cut in half by the same bomb. The owner stood in front of it, palming his bald head as he surveyed the unimaginable chaos of the damage. The upstairs looked untouched on one side while the other half was simply gone. His ground floor barbershop still had pictures hanging on the walls on one side and only a layer of dust on the chairs.

The man's wife clung to his arm, her eyes enormous and her mouth agape.

"What are we going to do?"

He shook his head.

I made my way down the street and over to the address Francis gave me, my eyes locating the bombed out house immediately. Heaps of rubble lay in the street, surrounded by the glitter of glass. In fact, most of the building's entire front wall landed on the street in front of it while the three remaining outer walls looked still reasonably stable.

As I began shoveling debris, a crunch from inside the house caught my attention and I looked over my shoulder. Two men were in the upstairs bedroom, one going through a chest of drawers while the other emptied the contents of a jewelry box into a bag.

Bloody looting scavengers.

"Oy!" I shouted up at them. "I see you, you rotters!"

The thief at the chest of drawers looked over his shoulder and we locked eyes.

It was Roy.

He shoved some stockings and a few other items into a bag and disappeared out a window on the opposite side of the building, his accomplice joining him in a hurry.

I dashed to the side of the building, yelling at them to stop where they were, but when I got to the other side, they weren't there. They'd simply disappeared.

Just then, I heard a sound from above me. The two hadn't climbed down from the window—they'd climbed up to the roof and the jewelry thief tossed his bag of stolen goods onto the roof of the next building over. Roy did the same.

"Oy! Stop!" I shouted again. "Someone call the police!"

The other man took a running start and then leapt the distance between the buildings. Roy looked down at me before his own jump, his eyes angry.

"Don't!" I screamed.

My stomach lurched as he sailed through the air, landing roughly and stumbling on the other roof. The two disappeared from view again and I ran back to the street, trying to spot them from there.

They were gone.

I ran a hand through my hair and cursed.

So that's what Roy is up to these days.

Cursing again, I grabbed my shovel and began the long cleanup process. I focused on my anger as I cleared the pavement, my knuckles going white as I gripped the shovel's handle.

Roy turned to looting bombed out houses in order to survive. I hadn't recognized the other bloke, but he looked right at home stuffing someone else's belongings into his pockets.

I sighed loudly and went about my work, my jaw clenched and my shoulder aching.

Perfect. Something else I can't tell Maisie.

"Sir?"

I whipped around so fast, I nearly hit the police officer with my shovel.

"Apologies for startling you. We received a report of a theft at this house not too long ago. What did you see?"

"Two men were upstairs. One got some jewelry and the other was…"

It was Roy Beckett.

"Um, the other was, uh…"

Roy Beckett recently deserted the Navy.

"He, um…"

Then he was a right prat.

"The other one was going through the chest of drawers," I finally said. "When I saw them I shouted at them to stop but obviously that didn't work." I pointed. "Then they got up on the roof, jumped over to that building, and I don't know where they went after that."

He nodded. "Right. Thank you for your time."

I watched as he disappeared around the corner. As soon as he had, I threw my shovel off to the side, the satisfying clang of it ringing in my ears as I cursed a few more times.

The moment I saw Maisie at the shop the following day, the words "I have to let you go" and "go back to Hazeldon" perched themselves at the back of my throat, ready to leap forth into the world as soon as I gave the go ahead.

"Morning," she said over her shoulder while wiping down some shelves near the front of the store. "I think we should change up the window display to include more toys and gifts for children since it's getting closer to Christmas. What do you think?"

I couldn't help but smile at her enthusiasm so early in the morning.

"Certainly," I said. "But can I have some tea first?"

She laughed. "Of course."

"You weird morning people," I said as I hung up my hat and coat in the back room. "You make the rest of us look bad."

Maisie laughed. "Hardly."

A customer arrived as I was bringing my morning tea back to the counter.

"Good morning. Let us know if you need help finding anything."

"Thank you," the woman said, wandering over to look at the camera equipment. She looked a little intimidated and turned to Maisie. "Do you know anything about this stuff?"

"I do. Are you new to photography?"

"My daughter wants a camera for her birthday."

"Well, we have cameras for beginners and seasoned photographers and everything in between."

As the two discussed the daughter's skill level and her needs, I opened the ledger to check some numbers. Going to the last row in the ledger, I noticed an entry I didn't recall adding. In fact, it didn't quite look like my handwriting either. It was tight like mine but still didn't look quite right.

Maisie was the only other person to have access to my ledger.

She must have sensed me looking at her because she looked up from the customer and smiled brightly at me, evidently not noticing any hint of suspicion from me.

I looked back at the entry and persuaded myself I must have been imagining it. I must have jotted the entry down in a hurry.

Still. It was unusual.

"Do you know if we have any film downstairs?"

I snapped my head up, startled from my daze. "Hm? Oh. Uh, I think so. I'll go check."

Jogging downstairs, I tried to push the nagging feeling out of my mind.

She wouldn't touch the accounts. She has no reason to.

I rifled through a few of the boxes in the storage room where we kept the extra film and camera stock, but I couldn't find any film. Before I went back upstairs though, I figured it would be worth the effort to try the photography developing room.

A line of drying photos hung on a string across the width of the room, a few of them still glossy with developing fluid. My eyebrows raised as I realized what the photos were of.

Several were portrait shots of two young and attractive women, one with light hair, one with dark hair. The blonde was also featured in a couple of photos at the end of the line, except she was posing provocatively, her dress unbuttoned in the front to display her chest.

I had a look around the few boxes of photography stuff we kept in there. It occurred to me Maisie hadn't mentioned a customer dropping off a film with *those* types of photos on it.

Carefully dipping my head under the string of hanging photos, I checked out some boxes in the opposite corner of the room. I sighed, realizing it was only more developing fluid. On my way back out, I noticed another photo hanging on the line, this one facing the back wall instead of the front wall like the rest.

I slowly approached the photo like it was a timid cat that might disappear around a corner if I moved too quickly. My eyes narrowed and my shoulders tensed.

It was a photo of Maisie and the blonde from the other photos. It was the side of Maisie's face—I had gazed at that face long enough to know it was definitely hers. She was adjusting the other woman's hair and someone took a candid shot when Maisie wasn't paying attention. Maisie was focused and serious. I snatched the still wet picture off the line, ducked under the string of hanging photos and compared them.

The blonde woman was sitting in the same chair as the other risqué photos on the line and her hair and makeup looked the same in all her photos so they must have all been from the same photo shoot.

Maisie used to take photos before her aunt died.

I blinked as the realization hit me.

She was doing photography again and using the shop's dark room and developing fluids for them. Maisie was stealing resources from the shop.

No wonder she wanted to stay. She's making extra money on the side. She figured she'd never get caught because I'm a chump, blinded by my feelings for her.

Maybe I was.

"Cal, did you find any film?" Maisie called down to me.

"No," I yelled back.

Shaking my head, I pinned the picture of Maisie back on the line with the rest of them before heading back upstairs.

The customer was leaving with a bag under her arm when I got back to the shop floor. Maisie picked up the clipboard hanging on the back wall behind the counter.

"We ordered more film a month ago. I'll have to check in with our distributor and see what the delay is." She tapped her nose with a pencil as she considered. "If we can't get more film through them, we'll have to find another distributor as soon as possible."

"Yes, it would be very bad to run out of film," I said flatly. "Photographers need film."

She didn't even look up from the clipboard. Not until, that is, I walked over and turned the *Open* sign to *Closed*.

She raised an eyebrow at me and smiled. Slowly her smile faded as she studied my face. "What's wrong?" She hung the clipboard back on the wall.

The genuine concern on her face nearly made my resolve weaken. Nearly.

"I just learned about your photography hobby."

Her lips parted slightly, and she swallowed.

"You took all those photos downstairs, didn't you? Except for the one you're in, obviously," I added.

"Yes, I took those photos." She tipped her nose up slightly and set her shoulders back.

A few pedestrians looked into the windows from the pavement, so I nodded to her and she followed me downstairs to the photo lab.

I thought she might shy away from the intimate photos hanging in front of us, but she just leaned against the wall and folded her arms over her chest.

The silence hovered between us for a moment.

"Why?" I finally asked.

Maisie's lips tightened. "I needed the money."

"Okay," I said. "But stealing—"

"Yes. I know. I used the shop's supply of chemicals and I use this room to do my own photos. It's true," she said. "I'll pay all of it back once this client pays us."

"I don't understand why you didn't tell me—"

"I was trying to avoid this conversation," she said with a dry chuckle. "And I thought you wouldn't approve of the photos I've been taking."

"I don't care about that," I said. "They're very good."

Maisie smiled at the pictures on the line, pride in her eyes. "Nora does the makeup and hair. She sews their outfits sometimes and I do the photos."

I stepped closer to her. "Neither of us make a fortune from working at the shop, I realize, but if I wasn't paying you enough to live on, you should have said so."

She winced. "It's not that. I just…wanted some extra money for Christmas gifts, that's all." She slid her hands into the pockets of her trousers.

My eyes narrowed. "Really? You could get in trouble for taking pictures like these."

She glanced up at me.

"I like them," I quickly clarified. "But some might not."

"We charge for the extra risk," she explained. "Our clients like to send them to their boyfriends while they're away."

The unusual entry in the ledger floated back to my mind.

"Wait."

Maisie's eyes darted to me.

I stared into the middle distance, the pieces coming together in my head. I slowly closed my eyes again.

"It's not for Christmas shopping, is it?"

Maisie didn't answer.

I took another step closer to her. "You made some changes to the ledger, didn't you?"

Her lips tightened. "Cal, I—"

I groaned. "What have you done?"

"I was worried about the shop staying afloat. The cost of everything is going up and now you have a second employee to cover," she blurted. "Yes, I've been putting my extra money towards the shop to help—"

"Nobody asked you to do that—"

"Of course not. It was my decision. I wanted to do it—"

"You had no right to tamper with the accounts—"

"I know that," she said. "But I knew the shop wouldn't be open much longer if I didn't do *some*thing—"

"And you need it to stay open to prove yourself to your parents—"

Maisie's eyes went dark. "Because the shop *means* something to me."

"Right," I said. "Because you believe it should be yours."

"Because *you* mean something to me." She turned around to face the photos, recrossing her arms.

I blinked, my stomach hitting the floor.

"Maisie," I said softly, "we…" I forced the words out. "We can't. I promised your brother I wouldn't, no matter how much I want to."

She spun on her heel, planted herself directly in front of me and placed both her hands on my cheeks. My heart pounded wildly, like it was trying to escape my chest.

"I don't care," she said firmly, her eyes staring up into mine.

Her lips found mine. The firm pressure of her mouth combined with the softness of her lips sent electricity through me and I greedily pulled her closer, my arms around her waist. Her fingertips felt like silk as they slipped from my face to the back of my neck. Heat grew between us as our tongues met, her body pressed tight to mine. She sighed into my mouth, her fingers tugging at the material of the front of my shirt as we kissed, and my blood raced at the sound.

She pulled her mouth from mine and I buried my face in her lovely, vanilla-scented neck, kissing and tasting it. She sighed again, the rhythm of her breathing picking up speed.

"We should… mmm," she whispered. "We should go back upstairs."

"Are you—" I kissed her neck again "—absolutely sure?"

She turned to face me directly. "I haven't been secretly putting money in the till so you can start slacking off during work hours."

I exhaled. "Alright."

She started for the door and reached the bottom of the stairs, looking back at me. "Aren't you coming?"

I gave a single nod. "I need a minute."

twenty-one

Maisie

My lips were still tingling as I jogged upstairs and returned to the shop floor, flipping the sign back to *Open* in the window. I felt flushed and jittery.

I'd done it. I'd actually done it. I'd kissed Cal Woodbury.

Thankfully the kiss seemed to make him forget about how I undermined his authority and tampered with the shop's accounts, but he knew I'd done it for the right reasons. I wasn't *really* stealing. In fact, I had done the opposite of that.

And there was a chance I would likely continue doing it. Passionate kiss or no passionate kiss, the shop was still not financially sound and I still enjoyed doing the portraits.

A few minutes later, Cal joined me on the shop floor, his cheeks pink.

"Feeling better?" I teased.

"Hush, you."

I bit my lip and grinned. I cleared my throat and straightened my shoulders. "Yes, sir."

"Now. About this." He gestured to the ledger on the counter. "Please don't make me hide this. You don't need to give money back to the shop. It's not a charity."

I frowned. He hadn't forgotten after all.

"But the shop—"

"Will manage," he cut in. "If we need to cut corners, we'll make it work."

I nodded. "Alright."

Several customers filtered in and out of the shop that afternoon. A few of them asked for items we used to stock but could no longer get because of rationing of, well, almost everything. I guessed that was about to happen a lot more often.

Late in the day, I was restocking a few scrapbooks near the back of the store and straightening up a few things when Cal wandered back to join me, clipboard in hand. He eyed the shelves and gave a hearty nod.

"Yes, yes. Jolly good work on these shelves, Miss Beckett," he said, doing a terrible BBC News voice. "Really topping work."

I shook my head at him, giggling. "Why thank you."

Cal glanced at the front windows. "There's something on this shelf I need you to attend to though." He nodded to the shelf behind us and as soon as I turned around to face him, he slipped a hand around my waist, pulled me to him and pressed his lips to mine. I wrapped my arms around his neck and matched the fervor of his mouth with mine. I felt my back bump into the shelf I'd been tidying, and I chuckled against Cal's cheek, nuzzling my nose against the stubble along his jaw.

"You've been distracting me since the day you walked in here," he whispered before pressing his lips to my neck.

It felt magnificent. My faint sighs were soon smothered by his mouth on mine and I went weak as I melted into him.

The door bell sounded and we both froze in place, our lips entwined. We silently put some space between us, I quickly adjusted my hair and went to greet the customer. Cal stayed behind to tidy the shelf a second time.

I helped the customer, a middle-aged woman, find a birdhouse building kit for her husband for Christmas. As she was paying for the gift, Cal emerged from the back and the woman snorted.

"You're wearing matching lipstick." She rolled her eyes and laughed on her way out of the shop.

Cal wiped his mouth with the back of his hand, laughing. "Why didn't you say anything?"

I grabbed a tissue from under the counter and wiped the red lipstick from around my mouth. "Oh, god. Okay, perhaps the shop isn't the best place for, er, that."

He smirked. "Shall I go help you with some boxes in the back room then?"

Oh. Oh, yes please.

I sighed and frowned.

Cal gave a shy smile. "Perhaps a real date then? Dinner? Saturday?"

My heart gave a flutter. "That would be nice."

We didn't manage to keep the shop an entirely kiss-free environment for the remainder of the week. However, our stolen lip locks were kept exclusively to the office and the back room. I also made sure to keep my compact mirror handy and check my lipstick on the regular.

We closed the shop on Saturday evening and I hung up the blackout curtains. Cal arrived at my side as I was hanging the last hook and I rested my hands on his shoulders while he lifted me off the stool with ease, his hands around my waist. As he slowly lowered me to the floor, a look passed between us. A look of understanding. A look of mutual yearning.

We briefly parted ways so he could freshen up at his place and get changed and I could return to the flat to fix my makeup and put on the fancy frock I borrowed from Nora—a calf-length black dress with a bright red rose pattern.

I met Cal on the pavement in front of the shop later that night.

He beamed when he saw me. "You look lovely." He smiled up at my red rose hair clip. "That's quite nice."

"Nora made it for me from fabric scraps," I said. "I wish I had half her talent."

"But you do," he said as we began walking to the restaurant a few blocks away from Barnaby Street. "I've seen some of your photos, remember."

"I felt rusty when we first started out. But it all came back quicker and easier than I expected."

"Are you going to continue doing the photos?"

"I think so." I glanced at him, gauging his reaction. "You probably think it's a scandalous hobby."

"You've really got me pegged, Maisie. I'm a prig who despises photos of ladies in lingerie." He raised an eyebrow at me and smiled. "No, I don't think it's scandalous."

"Some would," I said, "but I'm glad you don't." I slipped my hand into his, intertwining my fingers with his.

He glanced down at our hands and flushed.

"I also don't think it necessarily needs to be a hobby for you," he said.

I looked at him.

"If you wanted, I mean," he added. "You wanted to be a photographer when you were younger, right?"

"Yes."

"What changed your mind?"

I glanced at him and then looked back to the street ahead of us. "Aunt Jean dying."

Cal was quiet for a moment. "Taking portraits doesn't seem dangerous like some of her nature shots though."

"I know that," I sighed and shrugged. "It's not a realistic goal. It's unreliable. No matter where I end up, I can always work in a shop."

He was quiet again. Thankfully we reached our destination and the subject was dropped. One step inside the restaurant and I was quickly reminded eateries weren't subject to the same food rationing rules as the rest of us. It was like the war wasn't even on. Couples laughed and chatted, their wine glasses full and their plates heaped with food. As we took our seats at a small table for two, the air was heavy with seasonings.

The meal was delicious, and the conversation was easy. Cal made me laugh and the wine made my insides warm. As we shared a crumble for dessert, Cal kept looking at me and then looking back down at the plate, a shy smile playing on his lips.

"What? Do I have food on my face or something?"

"No, I…" He laughed and shook his head. "I was thinking about our first kiss."

"Last month?"

"No," he said. "Our *first* first kiss."

"When we were children, you mean," I said. "I wasn't sure if you even remembered that."

"I would never forget that," he replied quickly. "We didn't see one another for years but I thought about that kiss a lot growing up."

I gave a quiet chuckle and put my fork down. "That kiss was not that impressive."

"Maybe not. But *you* are." His eyes were serious and deep.

Heat rose in my neck. No one ever looked at me the way Cal looked at me.

"I bet you were popular with the girls at school," I joked, trying to ease my nervousness.

"Not so much." Cal sat back in his chair. "I had one girlfriend after I left school, but I eventually learned she was…not very nice."

"What do you mean?"

He frowned. "She saw one of my seizures and it frightened her. She cut me loose soon after that."

"What a horrible, nasty shrew," I spat, attracting curious glances from patrons at nearby tables.

"I'm inclined to agree." Cal laughed. "Oh, well. She married an older rich fellow about six months later. We obviously had different visions for ourselves. What about you? Loads of boyfriends growing up I expect?"

"No, not really. Not a lot of options in Hazeldon," I reminded him. "I think I always knew I didn't want to stay in Hazeldon forever, so I never wanted to tie myself to anyone there. Mum and Dad expect me to go back and marry some farmer and live out the rest of my days in the village." I shook my head. "I don't see that for myself."

Soon after we were walking back to my building in the dark, slowly making our way with the help of Cal's torch and the white markings on the pavement. Before we even got to Barnaby Street the air raid sirens began to cry out over London.

"Bloody thing," Cal muttered, grabbing my hand and picking up speed. "Come on, we better get you home."

We reached the door in front of the shop and met Mrs. Martin outside.

"Miss Beckett, you better hurry up and get to the Anderson or I'm locking you out," she warned, waving a finger at me, a pillow under her arm.

"I'm going to a shelter with Cal tonight," I said.

I hadn't planned on saying anything of the kind, the words just sort of happened on their own.

Cal glanced at me, but it was so dark I wasn't sure if Mrs. Martin saw it or not.

"Suit yourself," she said, turning the corner and disappearing down the dark alley leading to her back garden.

Cal closed the gap between us. "Care to explain, young lady?"

"I'm sorry. I wasn't thinking." I laughed. "I just…I didn't want to be away from you. I wasn't ready to say good night."

It was too dark to see his expression.

I laughed again, uncomfortable. "You probably think I'm mad."

There was a long pause. "Did you really want to go to a shelter?"

My breath caught. "No."

The up and down waves of the siren filled the silence between us. Finally Cal retrieved his keys from his pocket and unlocked the shop's front door. "Go on then."

He locked the door behind us and I followed the beam of his torch across the shop floor, to the back room and then down the stairs to the storage room.

I stumbled over a crate in the darkness and laughed at myself. "Maybe I didn't think this through. I forgot how dark it is down here."

Cal picked something out of a crate near the door. There was a sudden rough scratch sound and a small flame appeared in his hand. Without a word, he went around the room, lighting seven strategically placed candles. He blew the match out and switched off his torch.

"You found candles," I said, perching myself on an upside down crate, "and you brought them here?"

He shrugged. "It's dark down here. It needed some light."

"How did you know we would end up down here?"

"I didn't," he said quietly. "I thought if I was very, very, *very* lucky, you and I might be down here together again."

The siren stopped and a few low pops sounded in the distance. I could hear my heart pounding, echoing in my ears.

I suddenly felt shy, despite having blurted out how I didn't want our date to end, like some kind of floozy. But now that we were alone together in a basement surrounded by the glow of romantic candlelight, I was unsure what to do with myself.

Cal reached into the box by the door again and pulled out two pillows and two blankets. He slid off his jacket, added it to the heap of bedding and smiled weakly at me.

"You can put those right here," I said, pointing to the floor. "I got a splinter last time from sleeping on the crates."

"You won't be too cold?"

I shook my head.

He tossed the pillows down side by side and lay the blankets down on the cement floor. I added my coat to the pile.

"You're very quiet and it's making me nervous," I said.

He smiled weakly. "Sorry. *I'm* nervous." He glanced around at the candles. "Maybe you should go to the Anderson shelter. At least there you wouldn't have to sleep on the floor."

"No," I said, closing the space between us. "I want to be with you."

Cal's Adam's apple bobbed as he swallowed. "You want to *be* with me?"

Just then, a sharp whistle ripped through the sky and an explosion shook the building, sending dust spraying down from the ceiling. Cal threw his arms around me, sheltering my head with his body.

I looked up at him, still cradled in his arms, an unexpected sense of calm settling over me. "Yes, I want to be with you."

Cal released his grip on me and we stood facing one another in that dark room.

"Maybe that's forward of me," I said. "But we could be dead tomorrow and I don't want to have any regrets."

Cal studied my face for a moment, his eyes searching mine for reassurance. He tipped my chin up with his finger and softly pressed his lips to mine.

I felt lighter than air.

His hand cupped mine and he brought it to his lips, first kissing my knuckles, then the inside of my wrist. He laced his fingers in between my own and his mouth found my neck once more.

"I could spend hours kissing your neck," he murmured, his lips brushing my jawline and as he spoke.

"You would hear no complaint from me," I whispered, my toes wriggling within my shoes.

I clung to Cal as the shrill whistle of another nearby bomb echoed in my ears, soon followed by a shuddering blast. The low popping sound of bombs exploding in the distance continued as Cal's knit vest was tossed to the floor.

His following kiss was hungrier, more urgent, and I sank into it gladly, my fingers fumbling with the buttons on his shirt. Soon his bare arms were around me. I was warm all over and my lower abdomen ached. I wanted him.

I stepped away from him, reluctant to stop kissing him for even a moment.

Slipping my shoes off, I turned my back to him. "Can you…?"

He carefully moved my hair to the side and pulled the zipper down a few inches, stopping to kiss the back of my bare shoulder blade. The zipper went down a few more inches and he tenderly pressed his lips to my spine. My breath quickened as he unzipped further before kissing my lower back. I turned around to face him, pulling my dress down over my arms, letting it fall to the floor and stepping out of it, leaving me in only my knickers.

"You need to catch up," I said playfully, arching an eyebrow while dropping my brassier on my heap of clothes and turning around to face him.

Reluctantly tearing his eyes from my bare chest, he yanked his undershirt off, threw it to the floor and came for me, greeting my lips with his and burying his hands in my hair. The sweetness of his mouth was intoxicating. Closing my eyes, I let myself fall deeper and deeper into the heated and profound sensation flooding every nerve in my body.

I pawed uselessly at his belt until his mouth curled into a grin against my lips.

"Having trouble?"

I laughed at myself as he took over from me and soon his belt and trousers were on the floor with the rest of our things.

"Have you done this before?" I whispered.

"Yes."

Something in my gut twisted as the image of him kissing another woman appeared in my mind. But perhaps it was better that he had experience because I certainly didn't.

We snuggled together under our coats, stretched out on the blankets. We took our time, kissing deeply and lazily while touching one another and learning all the secrets hidden within our flesh. I buried my fingers into his hair as he tasted my skin, my calves trembling, my feet arching and my heels digging into the cold stone floor beneath us.

When the moment finally arrived, Cal was gentle and thoughtful. The discomfort quickly passed and I pulled him closer, my body wanting more of him, to possess him entirely. Our hips kissed since our mouths could not, too preoccupied with moaning our ecstatic approval. Words did not do the feeling justice.

Our gasps were joined by the sound of dropped bombs and explosions somewhere in Covent Garden and I immediately looked to the ceiling, wondering if it might come down on us right then.

"Maisie," he said quietly, "be here with me. It's just us right now."

I nodded and instead focused on tracing my fingertips along the defined muscles of his back. I cupped my hands behind his neck and brought him closer to me so I could kiss him again. I never wanted to stop kissing him.

His shoulders, slick with perspiration, went tense underneath my palms and he buried his face into my neck, breathing hard. He stayed there for a moment, his chest heaving against mine. He smiled down at me and laid a series of gentle pecks on my temple, cheek, nose, and lips before resting his chin on my bare shoulder.

"I love you," I murmured into his neck.

He searched my eyes for confirmation. "Really?"

I bit the corner of my lip. "Was this a bad time to bring that up?"

"No, not at all." He chuckled, beaming. "I've loved you since we were kids."

We blew the candles out and held one another for the remainder of the raid, our tingling limbs entangled and pleasantly exhausted.

twenty-two

CAL

Having frequent dreams about Maisie Beckett was one thing. Waking up with her body tucked into mine, my arm draped over the curve of her waist, was another thing entirely—it was so much better.

It was, in fact, the absolute best.

The all clear alert sounded overhead and when I woke, I felt an ache in my side from sleeping on a cement floor. But when Maisie's soft, naked form turned towards me in the darkness, an instant hit of adrenaline ran through me. She snuggled in close to my chest, sliding her arms under mine.

"Do you think the Nazis could drop a bomb on that siren?" she murmured into my skin.

I snickered and folded my arms around her. "Don't know. Would you like me to go ask them?"

"Please do."

I kissed her forehead. "It's probably not even daylight yet." I had no way of knowing as the basement didn't have a window. It felt very early.

She shifted her frigid feet onto mine, I groaned, and she giggled.

"How would you feel about relocating to an actual bed? I'm told they're very nice when you actually get to sleep in them."

"Your bed, you mean?"

"No, Mrs. Martin's."

She pinched me under our blanket of coats.

"Yes, *my* bed," I said. "Also, ow."

She nodded, the tip of her nose dragging over the hairs on my chest. "Alright. You might have to carry me there though."

I slid away from her, stumbled my way to find the torch so we could get our clothes back on. Maisie covered her eyes and laughed, trying not to look at my very pale body.

Once I had my trousers back on, she lowered her hand away from her eyes. "I do need to ask you something though."

Moving the pile of her clothes closer to her, I turned around to give her an iota of privacy as she got changed. "Yes?"

"The last time I was at your flat, why didn't you invite me inside?"

I instantly tensed. I was relieved she couldn't see my expression.

"Because I knew if I invited you inside, there was a good chance I would want to kiss you, and I was still trying to keep my promise to your brother then."

Guilt pricked me like I'd been dunked in a bucket of nails.

"If he really has abandoned his post with the Navy and if he really is hiding in London, he might come and see you," she said. "If he did, would you tell him about us?"

Squeezing my eyes shut and grimacing, I said, "Would you want me to?" I glanced over my shoulder and saw she was almost done getting ready.

"Yes," she said, pulling her dress straps up. "He should know."

"What exactly would I tell him?" I slid my hands into my trouser pockets and strolled closer to her. "That you make the loveliest sighing and moaning sounds when I kiss your neck?"

"No, not that specifically," she said, eyes sparkling. "He should know we're, uh, we are…" She frowned up at me, her lips a firm line. "Are we together now? Are you my boyfriend?"

She turned away from me and gestured to the flaps on the back of her open dress.

"Are you asking me to go steady?" I pretended to consider as I zipped her dress up for her. "I don't know, Maisie. It's awfully sudden."

She laughed, sliding her arms around my middle. "Let's go to your flat before I change my mind."

It was still dark when we arrived at my building and there were a few instances where I nearly fell off the edge of the pavement.

"I never thought I would miss street lamps as much as I do," I said as we finally reached the building's front door.

Once we were back at my flat, I tossed my keys on the small table by the door as Maisie scanned my furniture, the pictures on the walls and the view from my kitchen window. Tiger was curled up in the corner on the couch and barely opened his eyes when Maisie stroked his ginger fur.

"He's grown so much," she said. "I can't believe it's the same cat."

As I hung up our coats, the memory of my fight with Roy appeared in my mind. There was still a nick in the coat rack from where it hit the floor when Roy shoved me into it.

I gave Maisie one of my shirts to sleep in and she excused herself to the loo while I slid into bed. I melted as the familiar heft of my blankets and contours of my pillow hugged me.

When Maisie appeared in my doorway wearing my shirt—unbuttoned entirely and with nothing else on, I might add—my desire for sleep evaporated.

"Christ," I blurted.

She giggled and placed her neatly folded garments on top of my bookshelf before sliding under the sheet next to me. Resting her head on my bare chest, she lazily dragged her full lips across my skin before looking up at me, her big, round eyes alert and mischievous.

Sitting upright, I took a moment to admire her in the dim glow from my bedside lamp. Her chocolate brown curls, all loose and wild. The curves of her bountiful breasts peeking out from under my cotton button-down. Her skin like snow and her smile like summertime.

"You're like a dream," I said.

I pulled her onto my lap and a thrill shot through me when she gave a little squeal in surprise. Maisie touched my face, caressing the top of my cheek with her thumb before kissing me, starting softly and tenderly. As the shirt slipped off her silky shoulders, I gently pecked the bare flesh it revealed. I buried my hands in her hair as our lips met again, wanting more, needing more. When her breaths became ragged and I could feel her grinding against me, I pulled my lips away.

"Should I, uh—" I nodded to my bedside table, tremendously relieved when she nodded eagerly.

Soon Maisie pressed her forehead to mine, our breaths frantic, matching the quick rhythm of our bodies.

Sleeping in late the next morning, I woke up to the sight of her heap of disheveled locks on the pillow beside me. I wondered if I should ask her to marry me right then and there. I wanted to please her at night, support her and make her happy during the day, and wake up to those dark chestnut waves every morning.

But first, breakfast.

I slid out from under the blankets, pulled on a pair of trousers, and slipped out of the bedroom, careful to quietly close the door behind me.

I froze. I hadn't expected to see Roy on my living room couch, Tiger curled up in his lap.

"Oh," I said. "Good morning."

Don't panic.

"Good morning." He grinned.

His clothes looked a bit rough and the short beard on his square jaw made him look older.

I blinked. "How long have you been here?"

"Only about fifteen minutes." He nodded to the small brass key on the coffee table. "You should probably have that back."

"Thanks."

The silence between us was painful. I hated it. On the other hand, the longer we didn't speak, the longer Maisie might continue sleeping.

I joined him on the couch, mostly to move away from the bedroom door.

"I wanted to thank you," Roy finally said. "I know you saw me that day at that bombed out house. You could have told the police but you didn't."

I shrugged. "I never wanted to see you get in trouble."

Tiger rubbed his head eagerly against Roy's hand, purring softly.

"Well, whatever the reason, thank you."

"Do you make a habit of stealing things from bombed out houses?"

"Getting a proper job wasn't an option for me at the time." He shrugged. "I'm done with that now though. I took on a different name, so my future father-in-law got me a job working on the docks."

My eyes widened. "Sorry, your what?"

A wide smile spread across Roy's face. "I'm getting married. That's what I came here to tell you." He paused, a little more reluctant to share the next part. "And I'm going to be a father."

"How is that possible? You were still living here a month ago." My mouth tightened. "You didn't stay in the flat when I was at work, did you?"

"No, not quite."

I sighed, putting the pieces together. "You brought your girlfriend here, didn't you?"

Roy smirked.

"In my bed?" I cringed.

He laughed quietly.

"You git."

"I would like you to be at the wedding next month," he continued. "I'd like Maisie to be there too so I'm going to talk to her soon and let her know I'm safe."

If Maisie is hearing any of this, I am a dead man.

"Her name is Lillian," Roy added, his face lighting up. "She's a great gal."

I smiled. "Glad to hear it."

"Speaking of gals," he said, "who spent the night?" He cocked an eyebrow.

"What?"

"You're basically whispering so as not to wake up your lady friend and you've barely gone five minutes without glancing at your bedroom door." He chuckled. "Plus, I don't think those heels by the door are your size."

"Oh. Yeah," I laughed. "Someone I met at the pub." I shrugged.

"Jolly good," he said, rising from the couch. "I'm glad you got over Maisie. I was worried there for a while."

I nodded, probably a little too enthusiastically, and stood. "I can't believe you're going to be a dad. That is wonderful."

Better to change the subject back to him—and fast.

"I wanted to wait a few months, but her father was, well, pretty insistent we get married right away." He cringed and laughed again. "But she'll be a good wife and good mother." He headed for the door. "I should get going. I'll let you know the date when we know it."

After Roy left, I listened carefully for any sounds coming from my bedroom—snoring, preferably.

I silently opened the door and peered inside. A wave of relief settled over me when I saw Maisie's head still on her pillow, facing away from the door, just as I left her.

But my stomach dropped when she looked at me over her shoulder, her mouth tight and her eyes wide with anger.

twenty-three

Maisie

Cal sat on the opposite side of the bed. It was the very spot where we made love hours earlier.

He reached over to touch my arm, but I pulled away and bolted to my feet, bringing the sheet with me and wrapping it around my nakedness. His hand dropped limply to the bed.

"I'm so sorry I lied to you." He winced. "I promised Roy I wouldn't get you involved."

I glowered at him. "I thought my brother was *dead*, Cal, and you went on letting me think that." Struggling with the sheet trailing behind me, I waddled around the corner of the bed and grabbed my things, holding them to my chest. "You let him *stay* here with you and you never said a word."

"If we'd been caught and you knew, you could have been fined or imprisoned—"

"Stop it! Stop making excuses for him, for the two of you," I snapped. "Get out, I want to get changed so I can leave."

Cal, his mouth tight, sighed and did as I asked, closing the door behind him.

I stared at the back of the bedroom door, knowing he was on the other side of it, and I wondered if I should pitch his bedside lamp at it.

How could he say he loved me while not telling me Roy was alive?

I quickly pulled on my dress and combed my fingers through my hair. I knew I must look a fright and I'd likely get some sneers as I walked home but I needed to be out of there immediately.

Throwing the door open, I grabbed my coat. Glancing down at my shoes, I recalled the exchange between Roy and Cal about who was in Cal's bed. Roy assumed it wasn't me because his sister would never just give it away.

But I had. To a liar. Twice.

My throat stung as I slipped my shoes on.

"Maisie, please don't be angry with me. I was only trying to protect you—"

"You should have told me." My throat caught, and I swallowed the emotions down. "You should have given me the choice. He's *my* brother. I deserved to know if he was alive or dead."

"But we couldn't tell you without the risk of you getting in trouble—"

"He's getting married and getting a job and doing this and that, so I guess the risk must not be too serious after all."

"Roy is doing a lot of stupid things he shouldn't be doing," Cal added.

Exhaling slowly, I faced the door. "When you actually love someone, you don't lie to them. You don't keep things like that from them."

"You know I love you though," he said quietly.

"I thought he was dead," I repeated. In that moment I wanted to hurt him. "Just because you don't care about your siblings, that doesn't mean the rest of us don't."

I regretted saying it immediately. But once the words were out there, it was too late.

Cal didn't say anything. I left without looking back. It was the second time I'd walked down that hallway with tears in my eyes. Once again, Cal didn't come after me.

"Maisie, darling, are you alright?"

Snapping out of my haze, I looked up at Mum. "Hmm? Oh. Yes.

I'm fine."

"You better eat some more of your dinner," Dad said from across the table. "We can't waste rations."

I nodded and poked my fork at some lukewarm potatoes.

The two of them exchanged looks. I pretended not to notice.

"How's the shop?" Dad added.

I felt the smooth metal of my fork as my grip on it tightened. "The shop is fine."

Well, not fine. *It'll probably be insolvent soon.*

Cal made me promise to stop putting my wages back in the till even though I was still doing the occasional photo session.

"That money is yours. You earned it," Cal had said. "All of it."

"Well, it's nice you could come for a visit," Mum said. "Are you just staying the one night?"

I chewed slowly. It felt prickly in my throat as I swallowed. "I don't know if I'm going back."

Dad's fork slipped across the surface of the dinner plate and it let out a screech. "Not going back? But it's the Christmas season. You have to go back. Calvin can't handle the Christmas rush on his own."

He and Mum exchanged worried glances again. I really wished they would stop doing that, like I couldn't see it happening.

"I think you overestimate how much money Londoners have to spend on craft and hobby supplies right now," I muttered, picking up my water glass. "A lot of them are preoccupied—too busy worrying about where they're going to sleep or if a Nazi bomber is going to kill them *while* they're sleeping—"

"Maisie, that is quite enough," Mum hissed. She blinked a few times, trying to comprehend. "Your brother would be so disappointed if he heard you talking about the shop like that."

I almost laughed. I was *so* close. Roy never cared about the shop.

Mum looked over into the living room, next to the stone fireplace, likely desperately searching for a change of subject. "I read yesterday there will be a shortage of Christmas tree decorations this year because of rationing." She let out a sigh. "I wish your brother could be here for Christmas."

"As long as he's safe, wherever he is," Dad murmured.

I looked at the two of them. They didn't know if their son was alive or dead. They were in the dark, as I had been. They didn't deserve that.

Putting my fork down on my plate, I took a deep breath. "Roy is in London."

I had never seen the two of them turn their heads so quickly.

Dad dropped his fork and Mum's mouth hung open a little.

I hadn't planned to tell them. If those two Navy officers came back and looked for Roy, my parents would certainly spill the beans. Not telling them, however, was the same thing Cal did to me. I just had to be careful about what details I gave them.

"Have you seen him?" Mum was leaning forward in her chair, her eyes wide.

No, not technically. But I did hear *him while I was naked in his best friend's bed.*

"No," I said. "I don't know where he is either. But I know for certain he is in London."

A crease formed between Dad's thick eyebrows. "He really did desert the Navy then?"

I slowly nodded.

His thin mouth tightened and he stared at the table cloth. Mum put her hand on mine.

"He is safe, wherever he is?"

"I believe so." I nodded again. "He's got a job and he's working under an assumed name." I winced. "And you're going to be grandparents. He's getting married soon."

Mum and Dad looked at one another, their eyes as big as the dinner plates in front of us.

Dad shook his head. "How do you know all of this?"

I opened my mouth and then closed it again. "I can't tell you that."

"Grandparents?" Mum repeated. "Married?"

"That's correct," I said to my water glass. "Her name is Lillian."

Her stunned, wide-eyed gaze landed on the middle of the table. "And she's pregnant."

"Yes."

I considered the contradictory thoughts going on in her head at that moment; my boy is a saint. My boy had sex before marriage. My boy is a war hero. My boy deserted the Navy. My boy is perfect. My boy is marrying a pregnant woman.

I dared not consider the names my old-fashioned mother might call a woman who slept with a man before marriage, especially now that I was one of *those* women too.

Dad cleared his throat. "Do you know if we can come to the wedding?"

"I don't know," I said, trying to ease into it. "That might not be a good idea because of the whole Navy situation."

"Right." Mum swallowed. She didn't say anything for a long time. "What is her family like? Are they Anglican?"

I shrugged. "I have no idea."

The table fell silent. Oddly enough, I felt a bit lighter then.

Mum abruptly left the dining room, sniffling. "Excuse me for a moment."

Dad exhaled loudly and rose from his chair, fetching a bottle from his liquor cabinet and two glasses. He poured one for himself and then placed the second glass in front of me.

"Thank you for telling us," he said with a stern nod before raising his glass to his lips.

I stared at my glass. My father had never poured me a drink before. That was always something he only did for himself and Roy.

Am I… the new favorite?

twenty-four

CAL

Maisie wasn't at the shop on Tuesday. Once again the shop was so quiet and strange without her. I missed the sound of her laugh. I missed the sweet smell of her hair. I missed the kind and patient smile she offered up to customers. Most of all, I missed the mischievous little smiles she shared when it was only she and I in the shop.

When I arrived at the shop on Wednesday to find it already unlocked, I heaved a sigh of relief. All was not lost. Not yet anyway.

She didn't look up at me as I came in, crossing the shop floor in front of her to deposit my coat, hat, and scarf into the back room.

"Good morning," I said on my way by.

"Morning." Her eyes stayed on the newspaper on the counter top in front of her.

I rubbed the back of my neck. "Shall I make us some tea?"

She coolly folded the newspaper and put it aside. "I have decided I will finish out the holiday season, but come January I will be moving on."

I frowned at her and sighed. "If you want to find something else before then, please do. Don't stay if you don't want to."

"It's not fair of me to leave you in the lurch during what will be the busiest time of the year for the shop," she said, her tone almost militant in its directness.

I studied her face for a long time, just to see if she would ever look at me. She didn't.

"You don't know how sorry I am."

She glanced at me for only a sliver of a moment before turning away to pluck the clipboard off the wall. Silently she went to the shelves to check on inventory, almost certainly to put some space between us.

Maisie was right though; despite the shop not carrying as many items as usual and despite everyone not having as much spending money, customers still kept us busier than I expected.

Between customers, Maisie began decorating the shop with paper snowflakes made from newspaper, hanging them in the windows and along the shop ceiling. If our country hadn't been at war, we might have found some tinsel and garland and added some holiday sparkle to the shop, but that just wasn't happening this year.

Thankfully the customers kept the two of us so busy that uncomfortable silences between us weren't too painfully frequent. I caught myself watching her from across the shop about a dozen times which I thought wasn't *that* bad, given how much I wanted to go wrap my arms around her and then drop to my knees and beg her forgiveness.

Around noon a man with his cap pulled low came into the shop, and I knew from his walk, height, and eyes it was Roy trying his best to stay incognito. He sidled up beside Maisie who was restocking a shelf.

Maisie wasn't supposed to know he was in London. I watched from the other side of the shop as she smiled weakly up at him. When Roy put his arm around her to bring her in for a hug, she flinched. For a moment, I thought she might even pull away. She noticed me watching them and nodded at me as the two of them went to the back room to talk.

I winced. He would tell her about Lillian, the baby, and the wedding. She would have to act surprised, like she was hearing it all for the first time. Or she would simply tell him she knew everything already because she'd been in my bed that morning and overheard our conversation.

Roy would surely clobber me if that was the case.

But no. Roy was all smiles when he emerged from the back room, touching the brim of his cap to me as he left the shop like nothing was amiss. Like he wasn't a man on the run.

It wasn't until a moment later I realized it was *my* cap he'd stolen.

It was near closing time when I finally got to ask Maisie about her talk with Roy. She was hanging up the blackout curtains over the windows, carefully moving the paper snowflakes out of the way as she pulled the fabric across.

"Thank you," I said quietly, "for not telling Roy you were at my flat."

She raised an eyebrow at me, her nose wrinkled. "Why *would* I? That's none of his business."

"I thought maybe if you hated me enough…"

I trailed off and shrugged.

She sighed. "I don't hate you, Cal."

That simple comment sent a memory flashing through my mind—my name on her lips as we worshiped each other.

"We can't be together," she continued, her gaze dropping. "I can't trust you."

A cold, hollowness rose in my gut.

The bell above the door chimed and, for a moment, I considered screaming at the customer to leave.

Before I could make eye contact with the customer, they sang out, "Darling!"

My head snapped up. "Mum?"

As soon as we were seated in the restaurant a few streets away from the shop, Mum beamed at me.

"That girl you have working at the shop is so pretty."

I hid my face behind the menu. "Mm-hmm."

"I didn't even know you'd hired someone else after the last couple didn't work out." I could hear the grin in her voice. "Do you always pick shop girls because they're cute?"

"What? Of course not." I put the menu down again. "Besides, I didn't *pick* her. She kind of just showed up one day and told me she was working with me."

She raised an eyebrow at me.

"It's Roy's sister Maisie."

Mum's face glowed with recognition. "You're joking." She laughed, startling the patrons at the table next to ours. "Goodness, you used to fancy her when you were younger."

I exhaled, frowning at her. "Please Mum—"

"She's grown into such a lovely young woman. I knew she would. Is she seeing anyone? Maybe you should take her out, see what happens."

"Yeah," I said quietly. "Maybe."

I really didn't want to get into it with her. Not then, in the middle of a crowded restaurant.

"I suppose Roy wouldn't like that very much." She sipped from her water and frowned at the lipstick left on the rim of the glass, wiping it away with the pad of her thumb. "He seems the possessive type."

"Yes, he's protective of Maisie," I added.

Mum looked at me over the rims of her glasses. "Not of her. Of *you*, my dear boy."

I blinked at her. "What do you mean?"

Mum sat back in her chair, her hands folded in her lap. "Even when the two of you were young boys, he was happiest when he was bossing you about. But as soon as any other child showed any interest in playing with you, Roy got so jealous. He didn't want anyone else to have you."

My eyes widened. "Roy isn't… Roy doesn't…"

"No, darling, nothing like that." She flicked her hand at me. "It was more like you were his favorite toy, and he was the only one who was allowed to play with you." She gave a little shrug. "Even when we moved to London and you made new friends he kept coming to see you, but he never wanted to meet any of your new friends, did he?"

I stared at her for a while. She was absolutely right.

She let out a small chuckle. "Did you not realize?"

"No." I felt my shoulders sag. "He made me promise I wouldn't date Maisie."

"And did you keep that promise?" The corner of her mouth crept up on one side. She somehow already knew the answer.

"Not exactly." I shrugged. "I messed it up though."

The waiter returned to take our orders, whisking away with our menus.

"Why did you agree to keep that promise to Roy in the first place?"

"He saved my life," I said quietly. "I could easily have drowned that day when I had a seizure at the lake—"

"Roy was a hero that day," she cut in. "I would never say otherwise. But how long are you going to owe him for that?" She rummaged in her bag for her Woodbines and matches. She lit a cigarette and blew the smoke from the corner of her lips. "It was such a long time ago."

She was right. Of course she was right. There were so many times growing up I went along with what Roy wanted me to do, only because he pulled me out of the lake that day. We were swimming together and then, suddenly, I was on the shore, coughing up water, Roy screaming for help beside me. Since then Roy had always been the one in charge.

It was my first seizure. A few months later, Dad moved out.

Dad.

"Mum, did you know I have half-siblings?"

Mum froze. She looked at me for a few seconds before resting her cheek in her palm. She took a long drag from her smoke, her gaze leaving mine.

"Did your father finally tell you?"

"No. My sister found me and told me."

She winced. Sighing, she closed her eyes. "Yes, I know about your siblings."

"How long have you known?"

"I learned about Susan shortly before your father left." Mum tapped her cigarette in the ashtray, letting the smoke curl and spiral in the tense space between us. "It destroyed me."

I remembered the sound of her sobbing for weeks after.

We were both quiet for a few minutes. I scanned the restaurant, wondering if anyone else there that evening was learning about family secrets while waiting for their food.

"Why did neither of you tell me I had siblings?"

Mum stubbed out her cigarette. "Stubbornness on my part.

Cowardice on the part of your father." She gave a small shrug. "They weren't my children to tell you about, so I left it to him. I wanted to tell you, dear. You must believe me."

I nodded.

"Have you spoken to your father since learning about them?"

"No."

"Do you plan to go see him?"

"No." I sipped my water. "He wants me to meet them but…"

Our food arrived. Exotic seasonings weren't plentiful in England during wartime, so the food was fine but not nearly as flavorful as it once was. I was mostly thankful the meals ended the Dad conversation.

"You're not spending the night in London, are you?" I asked between bites. "It's not safe."

She finished chewing her mouthful and sipped her water again, avoiding my gaze all of the sudden.

"I've been spending quite a lot of time in Peckham," she said, folding her hands in her lap. "My friend is picking me up in his motorcar after dinner."

I raised an eyebrow. "Your friend?"

Mum's face was painted with obvious guilt. I burst out laughing.

"You can say you have a boyfriend," I said.

She reached into her bag again, pulling out a plain silver band. She slid it onto her finger and smiled weakly. "He's not my boyfriend, actually."

"Mum!" I laughed again. "Why didn't you say you're getting married? That's wonderful!"

Mum beamed. "Thank you, dear. His name is Arnold and he's really a lovely man."

"I'm so happy for you."

I really was. She deserved to be happy. Once upon a time I held on to childish dreams she and Dad would find their way back to one another, but those days were long, long gone.

We chatted briefly about her upcoming wedding before things veered back to me and my less successful romantic life.

"So, you don't think things will work out between you and Maisie? That's a shame. She was always such a nice girl," Mum said.

"She's even taking another job after the holidays because she doesn't want to be around me anymore."

"Well, don't keep your heart closed up for too long like I did," she said. "You never know when someone else will walk into your life."

"Right." I nodded.

Except I don't want anyone else.

twenty-five

Maisie

Nora and I tended to another photoshoot on Sunday morning, giggling as our pair of clients hammed it up for the camera, wearing old Christmas tinsel we found in a box in the attic as a feather boa. Best of all, the clients were pleased as punch when they left after the session.

"Oh, I forgot to tell you," Nora said, folding the attic ladder back up into the ceiling once we were done, "there's a shoe store in Chelsea that's looking for a shop girl. The job is yours if you want it."

"Chelsea?" I sighed. "I'll think about it. I was hoping to find something in Covent Garden so I wouldn't have to depend on the tube or the bus. It's so unreliable right now."

Not that their unreliability was their fault—they couldn't help it the Germans continued to create huge chasms in the roads and deep into the earth every night. Although with the colder weather, some nights were comparatively quiet and calm.

"Right," Nora said with a determined nod. "I'll keep asking around. We'll find your something so we can get you out of the hobby shop. It'll be good for you."

I nodded. "Thank you." I leaned in the doorway of my bedroom and crossed my arms over my chest.

"I know you really liked him, Maisie," she added softly. "I'm so sorry things didn't work out."

"Me too." I smiled weakly, looking to the view out of my bedroom window. "Perhaps I should go back to Hazeldon. There are no bombs there at least."

"By the sounds of it, there are no men there either," Nora said with a derisive snort.

I laughed. "That might be for the best."

"Oh, don't go back to Hazeldon." She gave a little whine. "Would you be happy there? Be honest."

"Probably not."

"Exactly! Besides, you can't leave me alone with Mrs. Martin. I simply won't allow it." She turned her head sideways, listening. "Speaking of the old bat, sounds like she's back from church."

"Maybe she'll insist you go to church with her if it's only the two of you here," I teased.

"Don't even joke about that. That sounds *exactly* like something she'd do." She snickered. "I'd probably set foot in the place and burst into flames instantaneously."

"Should we buy her a Christmas gift?" I winced. "Is that something we're obligated to do?"

"Perhaps," she scoffed. "Why don't we go do a bit of holiday shopping and then go see a movie this afternoon?"

"Yes, please. Let's see something funny. I could do with a little cheering up."

When we got back to the flat late that afternoon, the air had an odd tension in it. Nora and I expected to come home to the sounds and smells of dinner being prepared, but it was silent. The wireless wasn't even on.

I exchanged looks with Nora and we set our bags down by the door. She looked as worried as I did. I slid my shoes off and started for the kitchen door before Nora grabbed my arm.

"What if she's dead?" she whispered.

I hushed her and we approached the kitchen together, Nora still clinging to my arm. Thanks to the Blitz, I'd seen plenty of dead bodies but had never discovered the corpse of someone I knew personally.

When we found Mrs. Martin seated at the dining table, the tension in my shoulders eased.

And then it came back as soon as I saw what was on the table in front of her.

Her eyes flicked up to us as we stood in the doorway. Her back was ramrod straight and a cup of tea sat empty in front of her. She'd been waiting for us.

"Good afternoon, Mrs. Martin," I said, my mouth going dry very suddenly.

Nora's fingers squeezed tighter into the flesh on my arm as she too noticed the large envelope on the table in front of our landlady.

That envelope contained the printed photos from the photoshoot we'd done for a client the Sunday before. Nora was supposed to give them to the client the following day.

"You found my celebrity photos," Nora blurted. "You must know I collect photos of famous actresses."

Mrs. Martin's head tilted, her eyes narrowing. When Nora reached for them, Mrs. Martin snatched the envelope off the table and out of her reach. I winced, seeing the angry creases in the envelope and knowing the photos inside would no longer be smooth.

"What exactly has been going on under my roof? I want to know, and I want to know right now." Her nostrils flared and her thin lips pursed.

"Well, to start, you've obviously been going through our belongings," Nora said.

I elbowed her gently.

Mrs. Martin turned the envelope upside down and the glossy photos slid out onto the table; three racy photos of a young woman—her dark, seductive eyes locked on the camera and her lips curled into a wicked grin. Her short dress only obscured the very top portion of her long, stocking-free legs.

I winced. This was bad. This was very bad.

"That's my chair in the attic."

Nora and I remained silent.

"I went up there this afternoon to get my Christmas decorations down."

Oh, bloody hell.

"I was going to ask you two to go up for me, but you were off somewhere doing God knows what—"

"We went to the cinema—"

"—so I climbed up there myself. Lucky I didn't break my neck, that's what I say. And when I got up there, I see photography equipment and a camera and *my* blue chair." She clutched her chest. "I don't even want to *think* what-what-what filthy and-and-and *diseased* harlots have been in that chair. That chair was a gift from my late husband and now it's been… corrupted by these jezebels."

"You weren't even using the chair anyway," Nora mumbled.

I elbowed her again.

"So I decided to have a look around your rooms." Mrs. Martin gave a solid, single nod. "This is my house, I can look anywhere I want to—"

"We're tenants. We have rights," I said, somehow sounding even less brave than I felt.

"You gave up those rights when you brought these floozies into *my* home." She shook her head, her cheeks puffed out a bit. "Taking pictures of these-these-these *loose* women—"

"They were just a bit of fun," Nora interrupted. "We did it so they could send them to their husbands overseas. It was nothing scandalous, we swear."

Except for the one trying to lure her boyfriend away from his wife.

"It doesn't matter what they were for."

"We won't do it again," I said. "We're very sorry."

I was mostly sorry we got caught and we wouldn't be able to deliver the photos to our client. That was the worst part.

Mrs. Martin's eyes narrowed even further. "Not here, you won't. Both of you are to find new lodgings by next Friday."

Actually, no. *That* was the worst part.

I gaped. "But Mrs. Martin, you can't—"

"I certainly *can*. This is *my* house," she stabbed the table with her finger. "I won't have two pimps running a brothel out of my own attic."

As soon as I saw Nora's mouth open to reply, I grabbed her arm and pulled her out of the dining room just in case she uttered something that would get us expelled from the house even sooner.

Once up in Nora's bedroom, she slammed the door closed behind us.

"That frigid old crone," she said through clenched teeth.

I slid my hands into my trouser pockets and leaned my shoulder against her bedroom window, watching the people go by down below.

"Finding another place to board is going to be rotten," she continued. "So many rooms to let have gone to people who have lost their homes to bombs." Her bed creaked as she sat on the edge of it. "Maybe we can find a two-bedroom flat for the pair of us. I can't promise it'll be in Covent Garden."

She was quiet for a moment.

"You're thinking about leaving London, aren't you?"

I looked back at her.

"Maybe this is some kind of sign it's time for me to go home," I said quietly.

Her shoulders fell and her brows pinched together in the middle. "But will you be able to keep doing photography from there?"

"Certainly. I have to transition from portraits to—" I struggled "—tractors and veggie patches and—" I hesitated again, shrugging "—meadows."

"Sounds thrilling," she quipped. "No, no. You must stay in London and keep doing photography. You're so good at it and it's obvious you love it."

I smiled weakly. "Can we discuss this a little later? We better go grab a bite somewhere. I have a feeling Mrs. Martin isn't preparing dinner for us tonight."

We ended up extending our evening plans when two handsome chaps in uniform asked us to join them for a drink nearby.

"Did you say your names are Floyd and Lloyd?" Nora said over the music.

Floyd, the more outgoing one, smiled. "Yeah, we get that a lot."

Nora smirked at me. "One for each of us, huh, Maisie?"

I shared a lively dance with Floyd while Lloyd was absolutely gone on Nora, pulling her close on the tiny dance floor. Floyd was lovely but I was too busy thinking about the slow dance I'd shared with Cal. And his smile. And our kisses. And the way his body fit mine so well.

Nora and I lost track of time, dancing and laughing and feeling the warmth of the spirits in our skin. We parted ways and walked home but didn't quite make it back to Barnaby Street before the air raid siren wailed.

"Bloody thing," Nora cursed, looking up at the black expanse of the sky above. "Bloody Germans!"

We ran as the siren rose and fell, leaving a shrill ringing in my ears. I followed Nora through the alley between our building and the next, going directly to the Anderson shelter in the back garden.

"You two didn't put your blackout curtains up in your rooms before you left," Mrs. Martin snapped as we opened the door. "We'll lose the war because of the two of you, that's what I say."

Just then, the high-pitched whistling of a bomb split the air and the ground shook beneath our feet. Nora pulled the door shut behind us.

"No!" Mrs. Martin exclaimed. "Go back upstairs and put the blackout curtains up right now before the Germans—"

"They're already bombing us!" Nora screamed. "Do you *really* think two little windows are going to make a bit of difference?"

I tugged her out of the shelter. "Come on."

"Do you want us to get killed? Is that it?" Nora continued yelling as I pulled her along. "All this because we took some silly photos? Bloody hell, woman, you're insane."

Moments after I shut the Anderson shelter door behind us, I heard the unmistakable sound of the door locking. I slowly looked back to Nora in the darkness.

"She's locked us out," she said.

I couldn't see her, but I knew she was charging back to pound on the door and shout at her some more.

"There's no point," I said. "Come on, we better get to a shelter."

"She's trying to get us both killed," she spat as we made our way back to the street in the darkness.

I considered taking refuge in the storage room in the basement but quickly decided against it, determining it would be too painful to revisit that room again just yet.

"I think the tube station is closer than the nearest shelter—"

A bomb sailed through the air and crashed into a building on the next street over, sending rubble and dust in every direction. Nora and I screamed and ducked into an alcove, covering our heads. We both took to coughing as the wave of dust reached us.

Of all the things to think about in that moment, I thought of Cal and hoped he was somewhere safe. It was going to be a very bad night.

Nora grabbed my hand and we ran, watching the road for emergency vehicles and the sky for bombs falling nearby. The air was already thick with the smell of fire.

An overcrowded tube station was a daily occurrence for many Londoners. But when I laid eyes on one that night, I thought I might weep for joy.

We carefully tiptoed over the rows of people, some laying on blankets and some leaning against the hard, damp walls. Children cried. Some people read books or played cards if they happened to be lucky enough to be sitting near a lamp.

Most simply looked worn out—tired from sleeping on the cold ground of an underground station every night. Tired of rationing every tasty bit of food. Tired of shortages of everything else. Tired of missing their young men. Tired of missing their children they had to send to the country. Tired of air raid sirens and dire news on the wireless. Tired of that bloody war that had only just begun.

twenty-six

CAL

When the all clear siren sounded, I jerked my head up—not from sleep but from a fog.

The very concept of sleep that night was alien to me and everyone else huddled down in the basement of our building. The bombs came fast and furiously. The Luftwaffe were probably helped along by the bright winter moon, nearly full.

I spent the last several hours wishing I'd grabbed Tiger before coming down. I could have tucked him into my jacket where he'd be safe. I knew he'd be hiding under the couch for days.

The whistling of the Nazi cargo falling to Earth and the low boom of bombs striking the ground were frequently interrupted by ambulance and fire truck sirens.

"It sounds like a bad one," said one of my neighbors to her husband. "I sure hope Betty is somewhere safe."

For the hundredth time that night, I squeezed my eyes shut and hoped Maisie was alright.

No one got up right away. Not a moment of rest was had so getting up from the cold basement floor seemed a rough task to tackle.

I struggled to my feet and helped a few older folks up before making the journey back to my flat.

Bed. I wanted to feel my soft bed underneath my aching torso.

One of my neighbors stopped in front of me and I nearly bumped into the man. He had stopped to peer out the narrow stairwell window, out into the darkness of the street.

"Sir?" I croaked.

"Two of the buildings across the street are gone."

"How can you tell?" I squinted.

An emergency vehicle with flashing lights flew down our street, throwing just enough light. Sure enough, the dark architectural silhouette was missing a huge chunk in the middle where two pre-Victorian era buildings once stood, structural carnage littering the pavement below.

I squeezed past him and some of my other neighbors, taking two steps at a time as I raced to my flat, praying I had enough power in my torch to get me to Barnaby Street.

I was far from the only one out in the street in the early hours, checking on the level of damage done by the damn Germans that night.

My breaths were heavy as I ran, tripping in the dark more than a few times.

As soon as I got to Barnaby Street, I saw stretchers and bloody bandages. Entire walls of had come down, revealing the dust-covered insides of homes. The buildings looked as if their skin had been peeled off, every tendon, muscle and bone spilling out into the street.

Standing among the debris was Mrs. Martin, silently gaping up at her longtime home.

I aimed the dull light of my torch at the remains. The building had taken a direct hit. Two-thirds of it lay in a heap of broken timber and stone. The ground sparkled with glass from destroyed windows. Among the wreckage were hints of what existed there before catastrophe struck; a chair with a missing leg, half a bed, pieces of store shelves and several cameras.

The front counter was mostly in tact but the cash register was thrown to the ground, either by a bomb or by thieves. I suspected the latter as the open drawer looked to be entirely empty.

I think I was maybe too tired to feel sad or angry.

"Mrs. Martin?" I said gently, knowing she must be in shock. "Are you alright?"

She reluctantly looked at me, as if glancing away would make what remained of her beloved home crumble to the ground.

"What?"

"Are you hurt?"

She looked back to her house and shook her head.

"Are Maisie and Nora still in the Andie?"

"No."

I glanced around at the people milling about the street. "Did they go for help?"

"They weren't in the shelter with me last night." Her voice was so small. "I don't know where they are."

My stomach heaved. The taste of bile rose in my throat.

No.

"What? What do you mean?"

Mrs. Martin kept staring at the building. "I don't know. I'm sorry."

My mind raced, a blur of curse words and frantic questions: why was she not there? Damn woman, where did she go? Would she have gone to the basement? Surely not. Why wasn't she in the Andie on time?

I slowly looked back at Mrs. Martin, trying to keep calm. "Were they late coming home? Did you lock them out?"

She blinked up at me. "I would never."

I knew she'd done it before but there was no use saying so. She would deny it. Besides, arguing with an old homeless lady in shock in the middle of the night, in the middle of the street, was frowned upon.

Pointing my torch at the alley that led to the back garden, I maneuvered around chunks of wall and pieces of furniture. Holding the torch in my teeth, I climbed over a shelf but the thing broke under my weight and I rolled down a small heap of debris. I coughed and waved my hands as dust surrounded me.

The Anderson shelter was untouched by bomb damage. Mrs.

Martin's veggie garden plots hadn't been so fortunate. I banged on the Andie door.

"Maisie, are you here? Nora!"

I cursed as I went to the rubble at the back of the building, trying to see if the stairs to the basement survived the blast. If they had, the impact of a stone wall falling down upon them—I didn't want to consider that.

Between the amount of broken beams and stone and the darkness, it was hard to tell how much of the building now lay in the basement.

"Maisie!" Cupping my hand around my mouth and aiming my shouts down. "Maisie, are you down there?"

Leaning against a bit of stone, I felt woozy. I looked down to see my torch on the ground. I didn't remember dropping it.

I must have had a seizure. Then, of all times. I cursed and tried calling their names again and received no response, fighting the fog in my head.

Struggling over the rubble again to get back to the front of the building, I saw an ARP warden was comforting Mrs. Martin, bringing her a cup of tea and asking her if she would like to come with him.

"No. No, I'm fine here."

"Mrs. Martin, you need to come with me. That wall could come down."

I jogged over to them. "Do you really think the remaining walls might fall?"

He glared at me. "Does it *look* stable to you?"

"I think there might be two people trapped in the basement," I quickly clarified.

He gave me a doubtful look. "If there were people in that basement when the bomb hit—"

"They could still be alive," I snapped.

"Cal?"

My name said in Maisie's voice was the most beautiful sound I ever heard. I turned to see her running towards me in the dark, Nora following behind her.

As Nora checked on Mrs. Martin, Maisie and I faced one another in the street, not saying anything for a long while. My arms ached to hold her.

"We spent the night in a tube station." She glanced at her landlady. "Mrs. Martin locked us out of the Andie."

"I bloody knew it."

Maisie looked back at the building. "I'm so sorry, Cal. You must be devastated."

I'm so glad you're alive.

I shrugged. "I'm fine."

"How can you be fine?" She shook her head. "You worked so hard to make it something special and now it's gone."

Releasing a long exhale, I looked back at the shredded pieces of Beckett Hobbies & More. "There are more important things in life. I'm safe," I said. "You're safe."

She looked up at me. I forced myself not to reach out and touch her lovely brown curls peeking out from under her knit cap.

"Maisie, we better get to a rest center before it fills up." Nora returned to Maisie's side and sent me a nasty glare.

"That place is going to be packed. Why don't you spend the night at my flat?"

Nora raised a suspicious eyebrow at me.

"At least get some sleep before you figure out what you need to do tomorrow," I continued.

Nora frowned at Maisie, giving her a meaningful look.

Maisie hesitated before giving a little shrug. "Are you sure it's alright? I feel like if I don't sleep, I'll fall over."

Nora rolled her eyes but didn't fight her friend's decision.

I nodded towards Holborn and they followed me.

"Is Mrs. Martin going to be alright?" Maisie asked Nora.

"No idea," Nora said. "Her husband is gone, her son is thousands of miles away, I can't imagine she has many friends. What did she have left but her home?"

They continued chatting as we walked. I mostly thought about how I might keep paying my rent, now that I didn't have a shop to work at. By the time we got to my building, the black sky had changed to deep navy blue and most of the stars had gone to bed for the night.

twenty-seven

Maisie

I hadn't expected to wake up in Cal's bed ever again.

When my eyes first opened that morning, I thought for a moment I had spent the night with my head resting on his chest. But no. It was just his pillow that smelled like him.

Nora snored on beside me as I slid out from underneath the sheet and put my outfit from yesterday back on. Except for a few things I left in Hazeldon, it was now the only outfit I owned.

As I got changed, I began making a list in my head of all the things I'd have to acquire; clothes and shoes and a new ration book. I didn't even own a toothbrush anymore. Or a hairbrush. Or makeup or soap. At least I'd brought my bag with me to the tube station so I still had my identification cards and some money—not nearly enough money unfortunately.

If I thought my eviction from Mrs. Martin's flat was a sign I should go back to Hazeldon, the whole building being blown up was an even more blatantly obvious omen.

I heard the front door open and close, keys jangling. Pulling the door carefully, I emerged, smiling weakly at Cal.

"Morning."

"Morning." He lifted the bag in his hands. "I fetched some scones. Would you like some tea?"

I nodded. "Thank you."

Sitting at his small kitchen table, I nibbled on a scone with a bit of jam while he put the kettle on. Neither of us said anything. Finally, he sat down with our teacups.

This is far too intimate.

I dusted the crumbs off my lips and suddenly rose from my chair. "I better get Nora up. I'd like to give what's left of the flat a look before scavengers take everything."

Cal glanced at my full cup of tea and then back at me. "Alright."

On my way to his bedroom he added, "Would you like my help?"

"No," I snapped. "I don't need any more of your charity."

His eyebrows went up.

I knocked on the bedroom door. "Nora, we have to go." I peered around the corner at Cal again. "I saw a telephone on the first floor. I think I'll go call Dad and tell him."

Cal flinched. "I, um, I already called your parents this morning before I went out. They're on their way to London."

My shoulders tensed.

"Oh." I exhaled and looked at the floor. "I see."

"I now realize I should have cleared it with you first." He rubbed the back of his neck. "Sorry."

Yes. You certainly should have.

"It doesn't matter," I said quickly, leaning my head closer to the bedroom door again. "Nora, are you up? We need to go."

"At least finish your tea," he said with a light smirk. "There's a war on, you know."

I shot him a look and rejoined him at the table again. I picked up my cup so quickly, tea almost spilled over the side.

"What did my father say when you told him?"

"He was quite relieved you're safe."

I wrinkled my nose at him. "Not about me. About the shop."

"Oh." Cal tried to recall the conversation. "I told him the shop was hit but he didn't say anything about it."

I put my teacup back down, a bit more forcefully than I meant to.

"Why aren't *you* more upset right now?" I finally blurted.

His eyes widened. "What?"

"Your shop is *gone*. You have to start over. Everything you worked for vanished in an instant and you don't seem to care at all." I let out an exasperated breath. "How are you so bloody cheerful right now?"

His brows pinched as he looked at me, his head tilting slightly as he considered this. He finally heaved an exaggerated shrug. "The shop was likely to close after the holidays anyway."

I stared at him. "But it's your shop. It's your life."

"No, it's not." He sipped his tea.

"I don't understand you at all." I sat back in my chair and crossed my arms over my chest. "I would be devastated. It's not even my shop and I *am* devastated."

A grin crept onto his lips. "Are you mad at me because it was my shop that was destroyed and not yours?"

"Of course not—"

"I'm just happy you're alive, you fool," he said, as if it was the most obvious thing in the world. "I thought you were dead. I thought I'd lost—"

"Maisie, are you ready to go?" Nora said from behind me. "Oh, sorry, I didn't mean to interrupt. Ooh, scones!" She grabbed one and took a big bite.

I slid my chair away from the table. "Quite alright. You didn't interrupt anything." I glanced over my shoulder as I grabbed my bag from the coat rack by the door. "Thank you for breakfast."

As we made our way down the stairwell to the street below, I fought the intense ache in my throat and the stinging at the back of my eyes.

The shattered remains of the building on Barnaby Street looked even worse in the broad light of day.

Mum and Dad were already there when Nora and I arrived. Dad was stepping cautiously around the caved-in area that used to be Beckett Hobbies while Mum stood watch, her hand over her mouth.

She wrapped her arms around me, kissed the side of my head, and squeezed me tighter and longer than I'd expected.

"My darling," she said, petting my hair. "You poor girl. You must be so shaken up."

"Hi Mum," I said, my face squashed against her shoulder. "Thank you for coming."

Nora, likely concerned for the pressure building in my head, stepped forward. "I'm Nora, the flatmate." She paused. "Well, former flatmate now, I suppose."

Mum released me and gave Nora an awkward little pat on the arm. "Do you have family in London you can stay with until you get back on your feet?"

"Thankfully, yes," she said.

Still poking around the wreckage, Dad took off his cap to wipe his brow. "Some thief has made off with everything in the cash register."

Mum shook her head, looking down the street. "We knew London was getting bombed every night, but I didn't realize how bad it was until we arrived here on the train. We must have been out of our minds for letting you go to London."

Let me? You two asked *me to come here in the first place!*

I exchanged a quick look with Nora while handing my bag over to Mum to hold.

Careful not to step on glass, Nora and I climbed over rubble to get inside the exposed guts of the building. It was hard to tell what was shop, what was Mrs. Martin's dining room and kitchen, and what was from the flat's top floor—debris from all three were mangled together.

Checking under the counter first, I slid out the ledger and blew the dust off the cover and edges. I tucked it safely under my arm and looked for anything else important.

"Calvin should be here, too," Dad grumbled.

"He's busy," I said, likely a bit too quickly. Nora and I exchanged glances again. "He's coming later," I added.

Nora pointed to the wall above the counter, seemingly untouched by the bomb—except for the large, obvious empty space.

"Wasn't there something there before?"

"Yes." I sighed. "A Spitfire model."

I wondered if Cal would finally deal with his shock properly if he saw the shop as I was seeing it then—a ruin of splinters. A gnarled pile of everyday life, twisted together with stone and dirt and wood.

Nora, her skirt gray with dust, looked over at me. "Any sign of your camera?"

"I left it in the attic." I pointed to a gaping hole in the roof where the bomb struck first before bringing that side of the house down with it, right down to the basement.

Dad glanced over at me as he cleaned grime off his glasses. "Are you doing photography again?"

"Dabbling, yes," I said. "I guess that's over now."

"Perhaps it's for the best," he said casually.

"Perhaps."

Nora looked at me with shocked eyes. I shrugged.

Dad approached us. "I found these magazines. They're probably—"

"Yes, those are mine. Thank you," Nora blurted, snatching them from him.

As she grabbed them, an envelope fell out from between the pages of one of the magazines, spilling its contents out on the filthy floor between them. It was the photos Mrs. Martin found the day before, laying at my father's feet.

My heart leapt in my chest and I froze.

Dad glanced down at them and then looked back at Nora. "Uh…"

"I collect pictures of celebrities," Nora said, kneeling down to gather them before he got a better look.

"Those are quite the photos," he said with an uncomfortable little laugh. "Oh, you missed one." He picked up a slip of paper that fell out of the envelope as well.

Nora went to grab it from his hand, but Dad studied it for a moment. He slowly turned to look at me.

"Dabbling, eh?"

He held up the card so I could read it: *Thank you for the wonderful photo session. Tell your friends! M&N*

He glared at me. "Maisie and Nora, right?"

Nora spoke up first. "No, I don't know what that is—"

Dad whipped around to her. "What exactly did you get her into?"

"Dad—"

"Maisie, what are those photos?"

Nora tried again. "They're—"

"I wasn't talking to you," he snapped, holding a finger up at Nora. "Maisie, did you take those photos?"

He'd seen them. He'd seen the little note we included with our photos before we gave them back to clients. He knew I was doing photography again. He likely knew from the look on my face before I even said anything.

I was just so tired of all the secrets and the lying.

"Yes. I did."

Nora's mouth opened.

Dad exhaled loudly, taking his time to consider his next question. "What are they?"

"They're portraits," I said firmly. "These women wanted to send pictures to their husbands and boyfriends who are fighting this war. I wanted to help them." I tipped my chin up slightly. "And I did."

Dad glanced back at Nora before casting his glare back to me. "Between you and your brother, I don't know where we went so wrong."

I looked away. I had to. The way he was scowling at me made me sick.

He marched by me, glass shards crunching under his shoes. "We're going to the train station and you are coming home with us."

"I still need to get a new ration book before I can go—"

"We'll deal with it later," he said, his voice low and cold. "We are leaving now."

"Dad—"

"Do you need to pack a suitcase?" He gestured to the crumbling walls behind us. "We're leaving."

I didn't follow him immediately.

Nora, her eyes glassy with tears, rushed to my side. "I'm so, so, *so* sorry. I went downstairs for a moment yesterday, saw the envelope on the table, grabbed it and tucked it into my magazines before we left. This is all my fault—"

I squeezed her shoulder. "It's alright. It's no one's fault. Go make sure you have a place to sleep tonight, alright?" I shoved the ledger at her. "Please make sure Cal gets this."

"Maisie," Dad shouted from my mother's side on the pavement. "Now."

We quickly hugged, and I carefully maneuvered out of the bombed out building, following behind my parents silently, leaving my London life behind.

twenty-eight

Cal

Why did I even bother coming here?

I thought maybe there would be more to find at the bombed out remains of the shop when Nora came to my flat the day before to deliver the ledger.

"Oh," I said, staring down at its dusty cover and turning it over like it was a relic. "Thank you."

"You're welcome." She shrugged and started down the hall.

"Wait," I said from my front door. "Did Maisie go back to her parents' house?"

"Yeah." She frowned, her shoulders slumping. "They're furious at her right now though. Her father happened to see some of our—" She quickly glanced around "—client photos and he went through the roof." She winced. "Well, he would have if the building still *had* a roof."

"Oh, god."

"Not good," she added. "Plus, her camera was in the attic when the bomb dropped so that's gone too."

I thought if there was even a slight chance I could find Maisie's camera, maybe—just *maybe*—she might forget how badly I'd mucked things up between us and forgive me.

However, the bomb damage was much worse in the light of midmorning instead of the middle of the night when I'd seen it last. Sure, there were *pieces* of lots of recognizable things under foot but almost nothing I could make use of. The small stained glass window pane in my old office somehow survived, still affixed to its wooden frame. I took that with me, wiping the dust from it with my shirt. Anything else worth trying to pawn had already been pilfered by scavengers.

I wondered if Roy had been among those thieves.

Just as I decided to give up and go back home to mope, I noticed a young woman in a WVS uniform standing on the pavement, staring into the abyss of my shop. It took me a moment to realize it was Susan. I hadn't seen her since I'd stormed out of the pub that day after learning I had half-siblings.

"Oh," I said. "Hi."

"Hi." She hitched the strap of her bag higher on her shoulder and waited for me to join her by the street.

"I'm so sorry about your shop," she said. "I know you told me not to come here again—"

"I was upset. I shouldn't have said that." I shook my head. "Besides, it's not exactly my shop anymore, is it?"

She smiled weakly. "I'm glad I caught you though. I came here to tell you Dad is in the hospital."

"What? What happened?"

"He was trying to help one of their neighbors get to their Anderson shelter and he got caught in a raid. He's got several broken bones and he's pretty cut up." She paused. "He was asking to see you again."

He probably got hurt on purpose so I would feel guilty enough to go see him.

"I have to go to work so you better make up your mind quickly."

I sighed. "Yes, fine, I'll go see him."

She gave me the hospital information and hurried off down the street. I yelled after her and she stopped to look over her shoulder.

"Thank you for coming and telling me, even though I was an ass to you before."

Her eyes lit up. "Of course. That's what siblings do."

Her grin looked so much like Dad's it startled me.

After stopping at my flat to get cleaned up, I took the tube to the hospital where Dad was staying, not knowing exactly what to expect. I'd been one of the lucky Londoners who hadn't needed to visit a hospital since before the raids began but I knew very well hospitals were overcrowded and understaffed.

Nurses with blood stains on their uniforms scurried about like white mice. As I made my way down the hall, howls of pain erupted from various rooms and I moved to the side as gurneys were rushed up and down the hall.

Dad's hospital bed was in a cramped room that was probably meant for four patients, but desperate times pushed it to twelve and only five actually had proper beds. A few younger patients were sleeping on mattresses on the floor while others, like my dad, made due with flimsy looking transport gurneys.

I almost didn't recognize Dad with the bandage wrapped around his head, covering one eye and looped around the bottom of one ear. He looked at me over his newspaper, squinted and then slowly lowered it to his lap. A small smile blossomed at the corner of his mouth.

"Why, hello there," he said before turning to the patient in the bed next to him, uncomfortably close. "This is my boy I told you about."

The older fellow, both arms and his neck in casts, nodded weakly at me, unable to do much else.

I wish I had a chair so Dad and I would be at eye level as we spoke, but there wouldn't have been enough space for a chair even if I'd had one.

"Hi Dad," I said finally, having a proper look at his bandages. "What did you get yourself into?"

"This is what I get for trying to be useful." He exhaled. "Never again." He chuckled at his own joke and then winced.

I slid my hands into my trouser pockets and looked around, suddenly noticing I was the only visitor in the room. "Am I allowed to be in here?"

He shrugged. "The staff are a bit preoccupied to be worried about visitors right now."

"I suppose so."

Neither of us said anything for a while.

"Do you know how long you'll be here?" I asked.

"Not long, I'm sure. There are a lot of people hurt much worse than I am that could use the bed." He looked over at his friend. "Isn't that right?"

His "friend" glowered at him, but Dad didn't notice.

"How's the shop doing?"

"Blown to smithereens."

"Oh," he said. "That's a shame. I'm sorry."

Dad pulled himself up higher in bed, wincing again. "I need to get out of this bed for a few minutes before the nurse comes to yell at me for being a layabout."

I helped him out of the gurney, his arm around my shoulder. He felt thin. Smaller than I'd remembered. With his robe tied and his slippers on, we slowly made our way to the end of the hall where we could admire the view of the industrial building next door from two large windows. He sounded out of breath when we reached them.

"Is your eye alright?" I peered at the bandage on his head.

"Swollen shut at the moment," he said. "A chunk of glass came close to taking the eye, but I'm told it'll be alright."

I nodded. "Good. You're lucky." I watched shadows of people moving about in front of the windows of the building next door. Anything to not have to look directly at the man I'd been avoiding—and who avoided me in return—for half my life.

Dad cleared his throat. "You met Susan."

I didn't look at him. "Yes."

"And she told you about the boys."

"She did."

The silence between us was highlighted by chaotic sounds of the hospital ward behind us.

"I should have told you a long time ago."

"Yes, you should have," I scoffed, glaring at him. "You should have told me I had a sister. You should have told me I had not one but *two* brothers."

"You're right. I should have. I'm sorry I didn't," he said. "You don't know how sorry."

I went back to looking out the window. It was easier than looking at his pale skin, the purple shadows under his eyes, and the bloodstained bandage on his head.

"Why didn't you?"

"Because I'm a blighter. I tried but I didn't want you to hate me," he explained. "The longer I waited, the worse it became. By the time the boys were born I knew I'd missed my window."

"I don't hate you."

"That's a relief."

"Meeting Susan was…hard," I admitted. "Confusing too."

Dad joined me in window watching. "What do you mean?"

"When you left I knew about Ada, but I thought part of it was…" I felt my throat clench. "I thought maybe it was because I was seeing so many doctors around that time and—"

"Oh, no," Dad said. "Oh, my boy. Of course not. Me leaving had nothing to do with your seizures. I thought about staying longer *because* you were seeing doctors. No, it had nothing to do with that whatsoever. Is that what you've thought all these years?"

I shrugged.

"God. No wonder you have such a low opinion of me."

We were silent again for a few minutes.

"Your mother is strong. So much stronger than me. I knew the two of you would survive without me."

I rolled my eyes. "We had to move in with my uncle's family. You humiliated us. You abandoned your responsibilities—"

"I was miserable. Ada and Susan were my responsibilities too. I had to choose, and I chose to be happy." He shook his head. "I can't expect you could understand unless you've been in love."

"But you must have loved Mum once."

"I thought I did." He sighed. "We were young. Too young probably. By the time we grew up, we already had a baby and a home. You were the light of our lives and, for a while, I thought it was enough. But then I met Ada."

His eyes softened as he said her name and his smile was warm and loving. I couldn't remember Dad's face looking so perfectly besotted in my childhood.

And I think, in that moment, I understood.

Ada was *his* Maisie. He'd just met her at exactly the wrong time.

"There you are," said a woman from behind us. "The nurses thought you must have run off—oh. Hello."

Although it still stung to see Ada, it stung significantly less then. "Hello."

She was the polar opposite of my mother: shy, petite, and dark-haired with a youthful voice.

"I needed a walk," Dad said.

"Well, you'll have lots of time for that now. The nurse told me they need the gurney so you're coming home today," she said, glancing at me again before continuing. "I had a quick call with the boys to let them know you were in the hospital."

"Where are they?" I was surprised that I genuinely wanted to know.

Ada glanced at Dad and then back to me. "They're, um, they're staying with my cousin near Leicester."

"When they come back to London, you should meet them," Dad said.

Ada and I exchanged nervous glances at one another.

"Yes," I said. "I'd like that."

And I meant it.

twenty-nine

Maisie

"You're back from London already," said one of our regulars, a farmer who lived on the outskirts of Hazeldon. "You couldn't stay away, eh? You missed us too much?"

Actually, my home got blown up. Thank you for asking.

"Something like that," I said, forcing a smile.

Just like when I turned up at Beckett Hobbies and told Cal I was going to work with him, I went to the village shop in Hazeldon and told Doris I was there to work, even part-time if need be.

"Honestly, I'll work for free if I have to," I said. "I can't sit at home doing nothing, I'll go mad."

She raised an eyebrow at me.

"From boredom," I quickly added.

It wasn't the boredom. It was the uncomfortable silences between Mum and me. It was her disappointed looks and her general wariness around me.

"There are no photos of *you* in some negligee, are there?" was one of the first things Mum asked me when we arrived home after a painfully silent train ride.

"No, Mum. I only took the photos," I said.

"I still can't believe you would get involved in such a scheme," Dad said. "What on earth was going through your head?"

The store needed a little financial help to survive but I knew telling him wouldn't help.

"I needed the money," I said.

"Why? You had a job," Dad spat. "What, did you spend too much money on clothes or makeup or some silly nonsense?"

"No—"

"If you needed money, you should have come to us, rather than get involved with *those* types of women," Mum said.

"You're absolutely right," I said. "I don't know what I was thinking. Can we please talk about something else?"

The talking stopped but their frustrated scowls continued.

So I fled to the village shop, spending my day hauling boxes, sweeping floors, arranging produce, and working at the register. But then the questions came flooding in from customers, many of whom knew me since birth so weren't shy in the least.

"How was London? Is it as torn up as they say it is?"

"Why are you back in Hazeldon?"

"Did London not agree with you? No place like home, eh?"

"Are you happy to be back with your mum and dad?"

It wasn't until the end of the day, while walking home, that I recalled the faces I *hadn't* seen at the shop that day: young men. The only young men who came in were farmers, so they were to stay put. The rest were all in training or off serving already.

I wondered if the British army would ever get desperate enough to conscript young men who had occasional seizures.

As I reached the end of the lane in front of my parents' cottage, a young bike messenger stopped sharply beside me

"Telegram for you, Maisie," he said, handing me a card.

He sped away, sending a light spray of dust into the air.

My heart nearly stopped when I read the telegram.

Have been trying to contact you regarding serious matter. Please call when you receive.

-Morris Davies, Ministry of Information

Underneath was a London telephone number.

I had no idea why someone from the government would want to talk to me, let alone someone from the Ministry of Information. It didn't make a bit of sense. But that was definitely my name on the telegram.

How did they know to find me here*?*

It wasn't yet six o'clock. I thought, perhaps, Mr. Davies might still be at his office.

My feet pounded the road before I knew fully what I was doing or why I was doing it. I reached the telephone box down the road, tossed some coins in, and listened to the rings. They seemed to go on and on and I was very close to hanging up.

"Good evening," a woman chirped on the other end. "Mr. Davies' office."

"Hello," I said, panting a bit from the short run. "I'm looking to speak to Mr. Davies. I received a telegram from him—"

"Who is calling?"

"Maisie Beckett. I was hoping—"

"I'm terribly sorry, Miss Beckett, but Mr. Davies has already left for the day, but you can…" I heard a man speaking in the background. "My mistake. I'll connect you. Please hold."

There were two clicks followed by a deep and tired voice.

"Good evening, Miss Beckett," Mr. Davies said in a distinguished London accent. "You're a difficult woman to get in touch with."

"Yes, well, the Nazis found it appropriate to drop a bomb on my flat so I'm back with my parents for the time being."

"Yes, they seem to be doing that a lot lately. It's quite inconvenient," he said, his dry sense of humor appealing to me at once. "Miss Beckett, I'd like to talk to you about photography."

My stomach tightened.

"Oh?"

"I believe you recently met a friend of mine," he said before lowering his voice slightly. "Ruth?"

"Oh. Yes." And then it clicked. He was Ruth's boyfriend who was so busy with his job…and his wife. "Oh! Yes. Ruth. Of course."

"Our mutual friend recommended you so highly I thought I might contact you."

I blinked. *Is this man about to ask me to take risqué photos of him, too?*

"She mentioned you made her feel far more comfortable than any male photographer she ever worked with, you see," he said. "The Ministry is preparing a rather large promotional campaign to get more women involved with war work—volunteering, working at munitions factories across Britain, that sort of thing—and we're on the hunt for a few photographers to take portraits of women on the job. These photos would be used in magazines, on posters, newspapers, all over the place. We want these pictures to inspire young ladies to be enthusiastic about filling in while the boys are away, you see."

I stared into the middle distance, not quite believing my ears but hoping with every bone in my body that I understood. I was gripping the phone so hard it's a miracle it didn't crack under the pressure.

"Are you offering *me* a job?"

He laughed. "Yes, Miss Beckett, I am. Would that sort of work interest you? It would involve a fair amount of traveling—"

"Yes," I blurted. "Yes, I would like the job very, very much."

He chuckled again. "Brilliant! I'll send you some paperwork and a few more details about what we have in mind for the job and the campaign. And, because it's the government, a background check will have to be done but I expect you would start early in the new year."

"That all sounds perfect," I said, my vision blurring from the tears welling in my eyes. "Thank you for this wonderful opportunity. I won't let you down."

We said our goodbyes and I set the receiver down in the cradle, my hand shaking violently. I yanked the telephone box door open and practically ran back home.

I have to find a camera!

"Absolutely not," Dad said over dinner when I told him and Mum the good news. "No. I think you've had about enough photography—"

"A young lady, traveling all over the place alone to take pictures?" Mum shook her head. "Don't be daft, Maisie."

My eyes darted between the two of them, waiting for them to laugh and tell me they were joking before congratulating me and wishing me well.

But it never came.

"This is a once in a lifetime opportunity," I explained slowly. "I would be a fool to turn it down. It's a way for me to help with the war effort—"

"If you were so concerned with helping with the war effort, you should have taken nurse's training or something," Mum said. "Not this."

"How did that Ministry fellow even know about you doing photography anyway?"

I swallowed. "His, um, friend was a client and she recommended me."

Leaning back in his chair, Dad crossed his arms over his chest, muttering. "Absurd."

"You really want me to stay here and work at the shop for the rest of my life?"

"You were happy to do that not so long ago, I'll remind you," Dad said. "You move to London for a whole month and suddenly you're too good for the shop?"

"No, it's not that—"

"We want you to find a husband and start a family," Mum cut in.

"We don't want you gallivanting across the country taking pictures," Dad added, "and getting yourself killed, just like Jean."

There. There it was. The memory of Aunt Jean joined us for dinner once again.

After Mum and I washed and dried the dishes in silence, I went on the hunt for some of my unused clothing she stored in the attic. Lucky for me, she was terrible at throwing anything away. I rifled through crates of holiday decorations, toys, and extra blankets before locating several boxes of my old clothes, some only a few years old.

I pulled out a few jumpers, buried my face into the wool fibers and winced. They all definitely *smelled* like the attic. I found a few pairs of trousers, a hat, several skirts, frocks and shirts. No extra stockings though and, of course, no undergarments.

With my box full of clothes in my arms, I noticed a trunk nearby with the initials 'JB' engraved on the brass hardware. Still on my knees, I put my clothing aside and shuffled over to the trunk. The spine of the lid crackled as I lifted it, the single lightbulb above me filling the trunk with light.

They were all Aunt Jean's things. Piles of photos she'd taken. Pictures of her at school with friends. Framed award certificates she'd received for her photography. A few pressed flowers. Her death certificate and the program from her funeral.

But none of these things caught my attention like the biggest item in the trunk. Tucked off to one side was a camera bag, coated in dust.

My eyes narrowed. Aunt Jean's camera was destroyed when she fell off the cliff that day. I wasn't aware of her owning a second camera.

Pulling the bag from the trunk I wiped it clean, revealing the gorgeous soft brown leather underneath, lighter around the edges from years of use. That was definitely the camera bag I remembered Jean having with her at all times. I pushed the stiff metal clasp and freed the top flap.

Inside, Jean's well-loved Leica III lay dormant, waiting to be taken out for an adventure again. My throat clenched as I slid it out of its resting place, tracing a careful finger over its various dials and switches. I took the lens cover off and peered through the viewfinder. The camera was in perfect condition.

It didn't make sense.

Opening the bottom of the camera, I tipped it and let the film drop into my hand. I ran my thumb over the smooth cartridge casing. What I held in my hand was a precious artifact from another time—the very last photos my aunt ever captured.

Leaving my box of clothes forgotten in the attic, I raced downstairs and threw my coat on.

Mum and Dad were listening to the wireless in the living room.

Dad slid his pipe from his lips. "Where are you going?"

"You shouldn't be going out so late—"

"I don't know when I'll be back, don't wait up." I let the door slam behind me and jogged down the road to the Hazeldon high street, turning right on Fillmore Road.

Pulling my coat tighter around myself, I knocked frantically on Mr. Barker's door while hoping I had the right address.

When Mr. Barker opened the door one of his thick white eyebrows raised, relief flooded my insides.

"Miss Beckett! Are you alright?"

"I'm sorry to show up on your doorstep like this at such an hour," I exclaimed, "but I'm afraid I need a massive favor from you—tonight, if possible."

Mr. Barker's eyes narrowed but there was a gleam in them. He looked more intrigued than suspicious. "How can I be of service?"

"Do you still develop your own photographs?"

Mum found me at the kitchen table early the next morning, drinking a cup of tea and eating dry toast.

"It's early for you, dear," she said, still using a cold tone with me. "What time did you get home last night?"

"Late."

She filled the kettle. "Where did you go?"

"Out."

"Okay, okay. Be mysterious then."

Truthfully, I barely slept.

Dad joined us soon after. He too was surprised to see me awake and dressed already.

"Morning," he said as Mum poured his tea. "You came home late."

I silently pulled a bundle of five photographs from the pocket of my sweater and spread them out on the table in front of me, not saying a word.

"What are these?" Mum asked. "Did you take these pictures?"

"No," I said. "Aunt Jean did."

Mum and Dad exchanged a quick glance.

"I found her camera in the attic last night. There was still film in it. These were the last five photos Aunt Jean ever took," I continued. "I took the film to Mr. Barker last night so he could develop them for me."

"That was awfully nice of him, especially given how late you arrived at his home last night," Mum said, her eyebrows pinched in the center.

The idea of me possibly being seen as rude to one of her longtime neighbors probably chewed at my mother's insides like a tapeworm, only because it could somehow make *her* look bad, as if *my* rude behavior was a sign of *her* bad character as a mother.

"He was happy to do it," I said.

"He's a nice fellow," Mum said. "Probably felt like he couldn't say no."

Dad didn't say anything. He stared at the photographs on the table.

"This is the order these photographs were taken in, by the way," I added.

Mum and Dad exchanged looks again.

The first three photos were stunning, highly dramatic captures of the Seven Sisters cliffs in Sussex. Ferocious salt spray bashed the chalky cliffside while the clouds curled above the ill-contented sea, encouraging its nautical attack.

They were exactly the type of photographs Jean loved best.

The other two photographs were of pastoral farm land. A sign in the background mentioned the name of a village I recognized but couldn't recall the location of. Thankfully, Mr. Barker knew exactly where it was.

I folded my hands together on the table. "How is it that Aunt Jean took photos of the cliffs, fell off of them, died, and *then* took pictures of a farm nowhere near those cliffs?"

Neither of them looked surprised by this revelation. Neither of them spoke.

"Mr. Barker said he found it so strange Jean died the way she did. He knew Jean, you know," I said, trying my best to keep my voice steady. "She was smart. She wouldn't risk her life for a photo—"

"She risked her life all the time with those silly stunts of hers," Dad snapped.

"If she was planning to do something daring, she *always* took someone with her though. Jean was alone that day."

Mum wrapped her hands around her teacup and stared into it. "We only wanted to protect you and set you down the right path."

Closing my eyes, I exhaled. "Will one of you please tell me how Jean actually died?"

The two of them exchanged looks again. I really needed them to quit doing that.

"Her car was parked on the side of the road at that farm." Dad gestured to one of the pastoral pictures. "She put her gear in the back seat, and then when she went around to get into the driver's side she was struck by a motorcar and killed instantly."

"The other driver was blind drunk," Mum added.

My chest felt like it was caving in on itself, crushed beneath the weight of the lie I believed for so many years. The lie my parents told me and everyone else in the village.

I slid my chair back from the table and crossed my arms over my chest. "Why?" I croaked. "Why would you lie about something like that?"

Mom winced. "You knew how she lived, Maisie. Jean wasn't—" she glanced at Dad, "normal. She was wild."

"She was free," I corrected, my voice breaking. "So she didn't live within the confines of *your* definition of what a life should be. She was gifted and happy. Is that *so* bad?"

"We had to get you off that path or we knew you'd end up just like her," Dad said, shaking his head. "The radical friends, the parties, and the drinking and the-the-the—"

"Lovers?" I suggested.

"Yes." He glared.

"We wanted more for you than that," Mum said. "What kind of husband could you possibly find if you followed in her footsteps? No man wants a woman like that—"

"You're obsessed with me finding a husband or working at the shop and doing *nothing* else!" I didn't mean to scream it. I couldn't help it. Taking a deep breath, I shook my head at my father. "She was your sister and you used her death to scare me away from doing something I loved…" I corrected myself. "Something I love still."

"Is that why you took pictures of those London whores?" he

asked, his eyes like ice.

"I took those pictures because the hobby shop was about to go under if I didn't bring in more money somehow." I spoke slowly and clearly. "If the shop closed, it would somehow be my fault and you would never let me live it down."

His back straightened. "That's not true."

"That doesn't matter now," I said with a shrug. "The shop is gone, and I've got a new job." I smiled. "I'm taking the photographer job."

Mum stared at me, eyes wide and unblinking.

"I'm finally doing something because *I* want to do it, even if it disappoints the two of you," I added before glancing up at the clock on the wall. "I better go. I've got work."

Neither of them said anything as I left. What was left to say?

Of course I knew they were trying to protect me. But the lie was too great. It hurt far too much. The betrayal was too cruel—not just to me but to Jean too.

Cal lied to protect me too. But at least *his* lie didn't change the course of my life for years. At least his lie didn't make me afraid of going after something I wanted.

thirty

CAL

Roy sat across from me at The Ox and the Crane, two pints deep already while I was still working on my first.

"I kind of always thought *you'd* be the one dragged down the aisle first, not me," Roy said. "It's strange how things turn out."

Sipping the golden brew, I gave a single nod. "You're right about that."

He sat back in the booth and glanced around the pub for the tenth time that evening. Roy was still technically AWOL from the Navy so looking over his shoulder was just a part of his life. Confident we were safe, he reached for his glass.

"Tell me honestly," I said, "would you be getting married any time soon if your girl wasn't up the spout?"

Roy nearly choked on his beer. "Of course not." He chuckled uncomfortably. "Don't get me wrong; Lillian is wonderful. We probably would have ended up getting married eventually but not now."

"Do her parents like you?"

He rolled his eyes. "They're not real keen on me, uh, doing you-know-what a few months ago and then doing you-know-what to their youngest daughter. I think her old man would have killed me if I hadn't proposed." Roy shook his head. "She deserves better. You should see the flat we're moving to after the wedding. Horrible. But it's all I can afford right now."

"This war has put everyone into situations they never expected," I said. "Lillian isn't the first war bride and I'm sure she won't be the last."

"Speaking of her parents, they're having everyone over for tea and cake after. You're welcome to come. Bring someone if you want." Roy raised an eyebrow. "Maybe that bird you had in your bedroom when I dropped in."

Rubbing the back of my neck, I exhaled loudly. "No, I don't think so."

"You can keep my sister company then. I doubt she'll have a date. She's back in Hazeldon and sounds miserable to be back there again."

I sat back and avoided eye contact, feigning disinterest. "Yeah? You've been in touch with her?"

"I mailed her details for the wedding and she wrote back. She's got a new job of some kind. Photography, of all things."

"Really?"

Roy raised a brow at me. "Yeah. She used to do photography with Aunt Jean all the time but then stopped after Jean's accident. I think it scared her." He took a gulp of his beer. "Anyway, she's got some gig with the government now. So strange." He snorted. "They must be really desperate for photographers, I guess."

I smiled. "Good for her."

Roy's brow pinched. "What do you mean?"

"She took up photography again a few months ago. She's very good." I shrugged and sipped my beer. "I'm glad she's trying to make a go of it, especially if it makes her happy."

His eyes narrowed slightly and he sat back, studying me. "Something *did* happen between the two of you."

Here we go.

I put my empty glass down. "Yes."

He paused. "What, did you ask her out and she turned you down flat?"

"No," I said firmly. "That is not what happened." Although my stomach was beginning to twist, I tried to keep my tone casual and confident.

I'd done a lot of thinking in the days prior to my pre-wedding meeting with Roy and decided it was time to be honest.

His jaw clenched as he stared daggers at me. "What happened?"

"Maisie and I went on one date and then I messed things up by lying to her about knowing where you were. When she found out I'd known all along and you'd been staying at my flat, she ended things between us."

Roy blinked a few times and drained the rest of his pint, setting his glass down roughly "How did she find out?"

"You don't want me to answer that."

Roy's eyes slowly widened. "The girl in your bedroom…" Closing his eyes, he massaged his forehead. "You have five seconds to tell me why I shouldn't beat you to a bloody pulp, mate."

"If that's what it takes for you to grow up, go ahead." I shrugged. "Beat me to a pulp."

He wrinkled his nose. "What?"

"I'm in love with Maisie. I always have been." I shrugged, the tension immediately loosening in my shoulders. "She's furious at me right now but I'm going to try to get her back, if I can."

"I told you—"

"I know what you told me, Roy." I smiled weakly at him. "You told me I wasn't *allowed* to date your sister. I realize that's the way it's always been with us—you're more of a leader than I am. You tell me what to do and I go along with it." I shrugged. "But this is different. And we're not children anymore."

"You bastard." His eyes were on fire. "I can't believe you'd betray me like this."

"You can be angry with me if you want," I said, shrugging again. "Believe it or not, this isn't about you. So, you can flip this table over and give me a black eye if you want but I'm still going to try to win her back either way." I glanced around. "It's a nice pub so perhaps we can go out into the street if you feel you must throw your fists about."

Roy sat back, crossing his arms over his chest. He tipped his chin up and continued to stare at me as he considered his options.

Eventually, he released a loud, exasperated breath. "She deserves better."

"I know."

He gave a sharp nod. "And if you hurt her again, I'll rip your legs off."

"That's fair."

thirty-one

Maisie

It was Christmas Eve and London was, despite everything, jolly.

Since paper and anything shiny was rationed, stores tamped down their holiday displays, instead making do with old decorations. Last-minute shoppers didn't seem to mind, keeping the streets buzzing with activity.

Carrying my camera bag and gas mask with me, I found the little restaurant Nora mentioned in her last letter, a street over from the seamstress shop. I spotted her in the corner, she jumped up from her seat and gave me a tight hug when I reached the table.

"This place is so busy," I said, slipping my new (well, new-to-me anyway) winter coat off. "They must have good food."

"It's fine," she replied quietly. "It's probably more to do with the other restaurant on this street getting bombed last week."

"Ah."

There were hundreds of things I missed about London, but the nightly raids were certainly not one of them. Despite the frustrated glares from my parents, sleeping in a real bed every night and not listening to sirens or explosions was a pleasant change.

She rested her cheek in her palm, her elbow propped on the table. "It's so good to see you."

"You too." I smiled wide. "How are things with you?"

"Uninteresting, I promise," she scoffed. "My aunt is happy to have me there with her, but I *need* to find somewhere else to live or I'll go mad. Not that there's a lot of flats available right now." She glanced at me and gave her head a shake. "What am I going on about? I didn't even ask you how your meeting went this morning."

I nearly burst at the mention of it. "I'm so excited! Ruth must have really talked us up. I start early next month. My first photo shoot is at a munitions factory in Staffordshire." I didn't even care I was rambling on. "Roy gave me his blessing to take his car which is great because I get petrol coupons and per diem since it's official government war work." I stopped when I noticed the weak smile on Nora's face. "I'm sorry. I shouldn't have—"

"Oh, hush, you," she replied playfully.

"Are you quite sure you don't want me to go back to Mr. Davies and ask if you can come with me? You were essential to our photography jobs. I don't mind asking—"

She laughed. "Don't you dare. I won't have him getting cross with you because I'm a jealous brat. Besides, I like my job here."

"When you have your own fashion line, *I* will be the one to photograph it for all the magazines," I said, our menus appearing at the edge of our table, dropped by a frantically busy waitress.

"If you insist." She picked up a menu and frowned at the options. "I hope you're in the mood for vegetables." She peered over the top of her menu. "Have you spoken to Cal?"

"Cal? I don't know anyone by that name." I raised my menu over my eyes to hide.

Nora pushed the menu back down with a pointed finger. "Have you?"

"No."

"Are you going to talk to him at the wedding?"

"I don't know." I sighed. "He *was* only trying to protect me. He just…went about it the wrong way."

Nora dropped her eyes to the menu, glanced at me, and then

looked back down.

"What?"

She lowered her menu. "When I took his ledger back to him? Oh, Maisie. You should have seen the look on his face when it was me at his door and not you. He looked so sad. Very pathetic but, you know, in a sweet way. I'm sure he's in love with you."

I raised an eyebrow. "So you think I should forgive him then?"

"Dearest Maisie," she said with a grin, picking up her menu again, "you already have. I can see it in your eyes."

After a reasonably good meal we parted ways, and I headed for the nearest underground station, taking the tube to Wapping, following instructions from the last letter from my brother.

Everyone was well aware London's East End, particularly the docklands, received a brutal onslaught of bombs since the very beginning of the Blitz. But in my mind their streets were only slightly worse off than central London.

I was so wrong.

Following the crude map on Roy's letter, I walked by entire blocks that were nothing but wreckage and dust. What I assumed were once rows of homes and shops were obliterated, entirely flattened by months of raids. I tried not to stare at the absolute desolation the bombs left in their wake, instead focusing on the scattering of snowflakes falling to the pavement in front of me.

My fingers tightened around my bag straps as I felt eyes on me. London's poorest district was made poorer still and I realized I likely stood out in such a place.

"Put your map away," said a familiar voice. "I know the way."

I halted, nearly hurting my neck by looking behind me so quickly. "Oh." I tucked the letter away in my bag. "Hi."

Cal smiled cautiously. His shoulders filled out his suit like a dream.

I missed him so much, it hurt.

"Hi," he said.

"Hi," I said again.

I winced. His subtle smile grew, reaching his eyes and adding little lines beside them.

We began to walk together.

"Did you get a new camera?"

"No. I found it," I said. "It was Aunt Jean's."

"Roy told me about your new job," he said. "Congratulations."

"Thank you. I'm looking forward to it," I said. "Lots of pictures of women making bullets and shells and plane parts, that sort of thing."

"I'm sure you'll be wonderful," he said. "Now, will they be fully clothed or no?"

I laughed, probably much louder than the joke warranted.

"This is the place," he said, pointing at a small church ahead of us.

Its windows were gone, replaced with rough scraps of wood, but at least it remained standing. Several buildings around it were not so lucky.

Our steps echoed throughout the old church as we made our way up the aisle. I forced myself not to glance at Cal, just in case he happened to be looking at me in that strange moment. Sliding into the second pew from the front I kept my eyes forward, locked on the waiting chaplain, his well-worn Bible in hand.

Lillian's best friend sat in the pew across from us. To keep things as private as possible and keep Roy safe, the three of us were the only guests in the church. Our parents weren't even there. I wasn't quite sure if Mum would ever forgive Roy for that.

A few minutes later, Roy and Lillian appeared at the church doors, hands clasped. Lillian, a petite young woman with a stylish blonde bob, beamed up at Roy like he was the moon and the stars. Roy kissed Lillian's gloved hand as they reached the minister, practically glowing as he smiled down at his wife-to-be. It was like they were in their own world.

I wiped a tear from the corner of my eye. I hadn't expected to see such an obvious display of affection between them. I assumed the wedding was a technicality because of Lillian's pregnancy…but the love and joy in their eyes was so clear.

It filled me with hope.

As they exchanged their vows, the memory of overhearing Roy's announcement to Cal—Lillian, the wedding, and the baby—crept into my mind. It stung, recalling those words and learning of Cal's lies.

He let me believe Roy might be dead. He should never have kept that from me.

But he was fulfilling the promise he'd made to my brother. So Roy was partially at fault as well.

What if I had *been told? What if those men from the Navy had come and I was forced to lie? What if they could tell I was lying to them? What if they forced the truth out of me?*

As Roy and Lillian sealed their vows with a quick kiss, I glanced up at Cal beside me and wondered if he missed kissing me as much as I missed kissing him.

We followed Mr. and Mrs. Beckett back down the aisle and I snapped a few pictures of the newlyweds in front of the church.

Lillian's parents' home was a few blocks away, a narrow row house where everything looked like it had been mended four times over at least.

As Lillian's mother passed out slices from the modest, ration-friendly wedding cake, she frowned and shook her head. "I had to beg, borrow, and steal to get enough eggs and sugar for this tiny little cake," she said in a cockney accent. "What a shame."

"It's lovely, Mum," Lillian said, kissing her mother on the cheek. "However, I *will* need to have the biggest piece."

Roy smirked and poured something from a flask into two glasses for himself and Cal.

The small house quickly filled to the seams once Lillian's three sisters arrived, all of them with young children in tow. I continued to snap pictures of the happy family gathering until my film ran out.

Taking a break from the chaos, I escaped to the tiny back garden. Lillian's parents filled every inch of available space with a veggie patch, but frozen soil was the only thing left of that now. I thought of my parents—friends with all the local farmers and always getting extra rations on the sly. Their lives could not be more different from Lillian's city-dwelling parents. It was possible their home wouldn't even exist the following day, let alone their little veggie patch.

"I thought I might find you out here," Cal said, appearing in the doorway, his hands in his trouser pockets. "It's mad in there. Do you mind if I join you?"

I shifted to the left to make room for him on the small step.

"They both look so happy," I said. "Lillian seems nice."

"I met her a few days ago. She's lovely." He snickered. "Plus, I think she'll keep Roy in his place."

"I'm glad to hear it."

After a long silence, Cal spoke up again.

"I told Roy I'm in love with you."

My pulse raced as I slowly looked up at him. "Oh?"

"Aye." His face was so calm but there was a gleam in his eyes. "He wasn't keen on the idea."

"Naturally."

"But I told him I didn't care. He can hate me if he wants." He shrugged. "I've lost a lot of things in my life. I lost my dad and my home when I was a kid and now I've lost the shop. I can deal with all of that. But I can't stand by and lose you too."

I blinked at him, not sure what to say. Cal had always been the quiet boy who grew up to be the shy man. Despite this he spoke so confidently, like he had never been more certain of anything.

"I was such a fool," he said. "Tell me what to do to make it right."

A light snow fell around us, and our breath came out in patches of fog.

I looked up at him. "Come with me when I travel for my new job."

The words were out of my mouth before the thought fully processed in my mind. But I didn't feel an ounce of regret once I said them.

"What?" He let out a surprised laugh. "Really?"

"Unless, of course, you'd rather stay in London and open another shop," I said. "I suppose we could write to one another and see how it goes or—"

My words were cut off when Cal wrapped his arms about my waist and pulled me against him, kissing me until I was breathless. Smiling into his eager lips, I draped my arms around his neck to steady myself, greedily savoring the electricity between us. He rested his forehead against mine and held me as a cool wind whipped through the back garden, sending the snowflakes into a dancing frenzy around us, twirling to the beat of my pounding heart.

As we turned to head back inside to rejoin the party, I caught sight of a lone Spitfire soaring above us, and I stopped to watch it cruise among the clouds. Cal looked to the sky while lacing his fingers in between mine.

For the first time in my life, I, too, was free to fly.

epilogue

Maisie

Cal and I spent a few days over Christmas in Hazeldon. Londoners were able to celebrate their holidays without the sounds of air raid sirens and bombs dropping since the Germans took Christmas Day and Boxing Day off. A lot of people stayed in their usual spots, just in case the Nazis turned up, and made merry within basement shelters and underground stations.

Rested from their break, the Luftwaffe returned right after Boxing Day. Cal got to know his half-siblings pretty well as they had a nice dinner before all six of them crammed into the Andie shelter in the back garden for the night.

That raid was nothing compared to the havoc that hit London a few days later when the Nazis lit the city up with ten thousand firebombs. They targeted St. Paul's Cathedral specifically, trying to set it ablaze, and they nearly did. But the mighty landmark survived while London burned around her for two days, pouring thick clouds of black smoke into the pale winter sky.

By then Cal had given his notice for his flat and we left London in early January, eager to flee the scarred and ravaged capital.

While rushing to get to shelter during a raid, Roy was struck by debris from a bomb blast and spent a month in hospital. While there, he was discovered by a Navy officer and turned in. Luckily for him his injury left him with a limp. He was sent back to the Navy but could only perform desk duty, safe on English soil. He only managed to avoid court martial because the Navy was so desperate for able-bodied men. To protect herself and their child, Lillian went to stay with family in the country and she and Roy didn't see each other for months.

Nora remained in London throughout the Blitz, too stubborn to find a safer residence.

From the moment I stepped into the first munitions factory with my camera, I knew I was where I was meant to be. I got to meet so many smart, brave, and determined women and listen to their stories before taking their pictures.

Cal managed to find casual work here and there in the area while I was busy shooting. We usually stayed at small inns when available or at boarding houses. We sneaked Tiger in with us though, tucking him deep inside Cal's coat.

Of course, we had to pose as a married couple or the inns wouldn't accept us.

But once summer arrived and, on a sunny day off, Cal put his grandmother's ring on my finger and we no longer needed to pretend.

acknowledgements

Thank you so much for reading *The Hobby Shop on Barnaby Street.*

If you enjoyed this book, I would appreciate it if you could take a few minutes and leave a review on whatever ebook retailer you purchased from.
Reviews are the easiest way to support authors.

If you would like to hear and get subscriber-only exclusivers, sign up to my monthly newsletter: **jilly.ca/subscribe**

Thank you to Colby, Mom, the rest of my family, Colleen, Geoff, and my lovely readers.

about the next homefront hearts book

The Germans pause their bombing raids on London but life on the homefront is certainly far from ordinary. *The Seamstress on Cider Lane* is a lighthearted and hopeful romance, perfect for fans of *The Guernsey Literary and Potato Peel Pie Society* and *The Last Bookshop in London.*

Gifted seamstress Nora Archer opens a sewing shop just as clothing becomes rationed and scarce in Britain. London's fashionable elites soon discover her remarkable talent for giving garments new life and her skills are soon in high demand.

Having lost his flat during the Blitz, Jack Parker is relieved to finally locate a new home. He finds himself living under the same roof as Nora, the spirited and enchanting woman he thought he'd lost, as well as Nora's protective aunt.

Despite her aunt's warnings, Nora can't help falling for Jack. However, the sweet and bookish teacher is from a different world and Nora doesn't know if she fits in or if Jack might be too good to be true. She can't deny the intense attraction between herself and Jack—and neither of them wants to.

When a struggling friend's desperate plea for help lures Nora into the dodgy clothing black market, she risks not only her business and reputation but also her blossoming relationship with Jack.

Will Jack and Nora's wartime romance survive when Nora's secrets are revealed?

THE SEAMSTRESS ON CIDER LANE will be released on February 5, 2024.

Learn more at jilly.ca/homefront-hearts

Printed in Great Britain
by Amazon

38496701R00121